A delicious kind of tension hovered in the April night....

"Now I *know* I make you nervous," Melinda's companion observed. "You've got goose bumps!"

They were standing at the far end of the deserted lawn. Melinda could hardly see the tall figure of the stranger looming in the darkness. The muted sounds of the party going on inside barely reached her ears.

"Don't flatter yourself." Melinda tried to sound severe but failed. "I'm reacting to the weather, not you, Mr. X."

Again came that wonderful laugh. "Mr. X! That's a new one. I'll have to remember that. It seems I've been called everything else in the book."

"You have my sympathy."

"Honey, I'll bet your sympathy is really something to see."

"That's hardly a proper thing to say to a stranger," Melinda said reprovingly.

"Is that what we are? Strangers? I was just beginning to believe we know each other quite well...."

D0805159

Dear Reader,

Aahh . . . the lazy days of August. Relax in your favorite lawn chair with a glass of ice-cold lemonade and the perfect summertime reading . . . Silhouette Romance novels.

Silhouette Romance books *always* reflect the magic of love in compelling stories that will make you laugh and cry and move you time and time again. This month is no exception. Our heroines find happiness with the heroes of their dreams—from the boy next door to the handsome, mysterious stranger. We guarantee their heartwarming stories of love will delight you.

August continues our WRITTEN IN THE STARS series. Each month in 1991, we're proud to present a book that focuses on the hero—and his astrological sign. This month, we feature the proud, charismatic and utterly charming Leo man in Kasey Michaels's *Lion on the Prowl.*

In the months to come, watch for Silhouette Romance books by your all-time favorites, including Diana Palmer, Brittany Young and Annette Broadrick. We're pleased to bring you books with Silhouette's distinctive blend of charm, wit and—above all—romance. Your response to these stories is a touchstone for us. We'd love to hear from you!

Sincerely,

Valerie Susan Hayward
Senior Editor

VICTORIA GLENN

Life With
Lindy

Silhouette Romance

Published by Silhouette Books New York

America's Publisher of Contemporary Romance

For my dear friend, Earlene Duvall.

SILHOUETTE BOOKS
300 E. 42nd St., New York, N.Y. 10017

LIFE WITH LINDY

ISBN: 0-373-08813-2

First Silhouette Books printing August 1991

Printed in the U.S.A.

VICTORIA GLENN,

an award-winning writer herself, comes from a family of writers. She makes her home in the Connecticut countryside, but divides her time between the East and West Coasts. She considers it essential to the creative process to visit the Disneyland theme park at least twice a year.

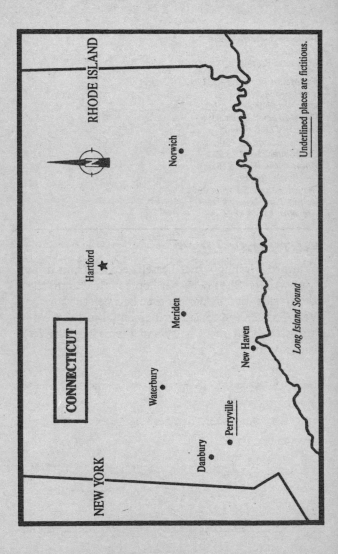

Underlined places are fictitious.

Prologue

Once Upon a Time...

It was a dark, stormy night, and the only house on the desolate country road was a stone monstrosity that might have belonged to Dr. Frankenstein. Joanna Prescott gave an involuntary shiver as the cold rain pelted through the thin silk of her summer dress. Nervously she rang the doorbell again.

Suddenly the massive old front door creaked open and Joanna was faced with three pairs of blue eyes staring up impudently at her.

"Who are you?" demanded the first towheaded gnome.

"What do you want?" interrogated the second.

"Where's your umbrella?" accused the third.

"My car broke down," Joanna began. "Could I please use your phone?"

"Our father doesn't like company," decided Gareth Clarke with all the superiority of a ten-year-old. "'Specially not *ladies.*"

"Yeah, and that includes *you!*" agreed Wyler Clarke, aged eight and freckled beyond belief.

"He's in the lab working on his 'speriments," seven-year-old Devlin Clarke added ominously. "He's a mad scientist!"

Joanna rolled her eyes impatiently. Surely she could handle three unruly little boys. Wasn't she Joanna Prescott, the daredevil journalist who had covered earthquakes, guerrilla uprisings and airplane hijackings? "I need to use your phone," she repeated in her most authoritative tone. It was a tone that had never failed to work with pompous dictators and military brass. It had won her the Pulitzer Prize at the ripe old age of thirty-one.

Mystified, the three shaggy-haired imps stepped back from the door, and Joanna strode purposefully into the cavernous hallway. The furniture was dark mahogany, the walls gloomy, and everywhere stood stacks and stacks of books covered with dust.

"There's the phone." Gareth pointed to an old-fashioned black box mounted on the wall. "It doesn't work."

"It never works," Wyler added loftily.

"Why didn't you say so in the first place?" Joanna threw her hands up in utter frustration.

"You didn't ask if it *worked.*"

If only I had a Ping-Pong paddle, she thought irritably as the three little gnomes began to convulse with laughter.

Suddenly there was a loud crash as a heavy door was thrust open, and something tall, dark and wild-eyed burst into the room.

"What in heaven's name are you boys up to *now?*" his voice thundered, and abruptly stopped as he noticed the new arrival.

"I beg your pardon," Joanna interjected. "I stopped by to use your phone." And all at once, the mad scientist didn't seem quite so terrifying. At second glance, he was as blond as his sons underneath a layer of soot, and those bright blue eyes were not wild at all. In fact, they were rather devastating.

"The phone?" Dr. Steven Clarke stared at the vision in lavender silk and was instantly self-conscious. Awkwardly he pulled off his horn-rimmed glasses and adjusted his grimy, disheveled lab coat. "I'm afraid it doesn't work. I never quite remember about the bill."

"Oh?" Joanna murmured, unconcerned. What an uncommonly attractive man!

"That is, I *pay* the bill. I just forget to *mail* it." He paused. "You're soaking wet!"

Joanna shrugged. "Am I?" Strange, the only sensation she was aware of at this moment was something wonderfully warm and comfortable. It was a feeling Joanna had never experienced in all her years as the "Ice Maiden of Journalism."

Dr. Clarke gave a shy half smile and reached out his hand. "Let's find some dry clothes for you right away, Miss—"

"Prescott, Joanna Prescott." A vivid pink blush suffused her cheeks as she took the proffered hand.

The man's grip was firm and strong. Joanna felt a tingle straight down her spine. Ice Maiden, indeed!

"I'm Steven Clarke." The mad scientist's voice actually trembled. It had been so many years, he had forgotten how soft a woman's skin could feel.

"Uh-oh," observed Wyler ruefully.

"Trouble," nodded Gareth. "We're in *big* trouble."

"Is she going to be our stepmother?" Devlin nudged his two older brothers.

"Why else would Dad be acting so silly all of a sudden?" Gareth whispered. "The next thing you know, they'll start painting one of our bedrooms pink, and we're stuck with a baby sister."

"No way!" declared Devlin.

"Forget it!" scoffed Wyler. "It'll never happen!"

Chapter One

There had never been a more mischievous little girl than Melinda. As a child, she had exhausted her parents, terrorized her older brothers and wreaked havoc throughout the neighborhood. Life, however, is unpredictable and people can change. Now, at the age of twenty-four, Melinda Prescott Clarke was a respected member of the faculty at one of the most staid and conservative private schools in New England.

The ultra-exclusive Perryville Academy for Girls was located on two hundred idyllic, rolling acres in the Connecticut countryside. Even today, as the late April sun began to sink behind the hills, Melinda marveled at the soothing serenity of the landscape. The faint green tinge of spring was everywhere this warm afternoon, from the exquisitely manicured lawns to the stately oak trees that bowed with ancient grace just outside her office window.

"What are you smiling about?"

Melinda turned away from her peaceful contemplation of the scenery. "It's such a lovely afternoon. Don't you agree, Selene?"

The petite young instructor who shared the same office rolled her eyes in annoyance. "Oh, please! Are you going to start with that Pollyanna nonsense again?"

"Excuse me?"

"What on earth is the matter with you, Melinda Clarke? Don't you ever get depressed like *normal* people?"

Melinda stifled a laugh. Selene Monroe had never made a secret of her resentment of her new colleague in the English department. It was a source of great irritation that after only four months on the staff, Melinda had become one of the most popular teachers at the school.

After a long pause, Selene added, "Oh, that's right. You never have anything to be depressed about, do you?" But there was more envy than contempt in her words. After six years as a somewhat undistinguished member of the faculty, Selene had found herself feeling more than a little jealous of the bright new arrival. It wasn't merely because Melinda Clarke was so well-liked by both students and teachers alike. It was far more than that. With her blue eyes, blond hair and winning smile, the latest addition to the Perryville staff resembled a cheerleader more than an academician. Melinda's all-American-girl good looks made Selene feel positively drab in comparison. Life just wasn't fair.

"Of course, Selene," Melinda said now. "I get depressed sometimes, like everybody else."

"I'm *sure*."

Melinda sighed and started to gather up the compositions she had just finished grading. What was the point of trying to argue with Selene Monroe? Ever since they had been assigned as office-mates at the beginning of the semester, the other woman had continually baited her in this tiresome fashion. But during her childhood, Melinda had been baited by the best of them. Her three big brothers, an unholy trio if there ever was one, had taunted and teased her endlessly, but to no avail. Melinda had driven them to distraction by her uncanny ability to remain unriled. And how often she had turned the tables on Gary, Devlin and Wyler with devilish little pranks of her own! Melinda smiled in fond memory. In fact, it was precisely those outrageous youthful exploits that had inspired Melinda's mother, a retired journalist, to create the cartoon character of Little Lindy. The rest, of course, was history. For over twenty years, "Life With Lindy" had been one of the most popular syndicated daily comic strips anywhere in the world.

"And what does 'Miss Perfect' ever get depressed about?" Selene's sarcastic voice intruded on her thoughts. "A run in her brand-new panty hose?"

"Gee, how did you ever guess?" Melinda almost bit her lip to keep from chuckling. There was no way she would permit someone like Selene to ruin her good mood. Life was just too wonderful right now. Besides, there was such a delightful evening to look forward to, as well.

Just then, the telephone on her desk rang. Melinda lifted the receiver and was immediately rewarded by a boyish voice.

"Ready for the ball, Cinderella?"

"Peter!" she exclaimed brightly, and was instantly aware of a glare from the direction of Selene's desk. "Actually I'm running a little late...."

"Sounds ominous. Can you still be ready at seven?"

"I'll do my best."

"Remember, I'm counting on you, Melinda. The firm's most important clients are going to be there." Peter Harrison sounded rather concerned.

"Don't worry, Peter," she assured him quickly. "You can count on me." In the three weeks they had been dating, the handsome young attorney had never seemed so tense. Melinda supposed it was natural. Tonight was an important stepping-stone in his ambitious legal career. A political fund-raiser at the home of Perryville's wealthiest citizen was not an evening to take lightly.

"Well, I'd better not keep you any longer, then." There was still a note of anxiety in Peter's voice. "See you at seven."

Melinda replaced the receiver with a contented half smile and reached for her coat and briefcase. Never had her life seemed so perfect and complete. She loved her teaching job, she enjoyed the special rapport she shared with most of her students, and she felt positively fortunate to have found such a charming escort as Peter Harrison. If only—Melinda stopped herself. What right did she have to complain? What did it matter if there weren't any magical sparks between them yet? That would probably come in time. Meanwhile, Peter Harrison was considered to be one of the most eligible bachelors in Perryville. He was extremely good-looking, intelligent and going places at the prestigious law firm of Caton and Henderson.

"You're going to the Kendall party with Peter Harrison?" Selene finally spoke up. Her tone was oddly subdued.

"Yes."

"Well, *have fun.*" The other woman practically bit the words back. Then, she rose from her chair and stalked out of the small office.

Melinda stared after her in utter astonishment. So *that* was it. Suddenly the reason behind so much of her colleague's resentment became crystal clear. Selene Monroe harbored a secret crush on the young man who had been Melinda's steady date for almost a month. And in that moment, she no longer disliked her irritating office-mate. Instead, Melinda felt an unexpected wave of compassion for the woman who saw herself as a rival.

Peter Harrison stood in the doorway of her apartment and whistled appreciatively. "That's quite a dress, Melinda. I'd say you'll probably steal the thunder from all the politicos tonight." The elegant, clinging black silk cocktail dress was more flattering than any outfit he had ever seen Melinda wear on any of their previous dates. He wondered curiously if the exquisite double strand of pearls around her slender throat could possibly be genuine. Of course not, the young lawyer assured himself quickly. No one could afford anything so expensive on a teacher's salary.

"I've never seen you this...dressed up before," he murmured finally.

"You look pretty nice yourself." Melinda smiled back. Goodness, she was thinking, he looked just the way she had always dreamed a boyfriend was supposed to look. At least in the movies. Tall, blond and handsome in his pin-striped suit. Oh, her three brothers were all good-looking men, but Peter looked like an actor. How lucky she was to have someone like him be so interested in her. Especially considering her past. Quickly Melinda cleared her throat. The past was the past. There was no reason Peter Harrison had to know anything about the endless misadventures of her youth. There was no point in revealing certain details of her somewhat rowdy childhood. Not yet, anyhow. The truth was, it had taken Melinda years to live down her image as Little Lindy, the real-life inspiration for a cartoon character known affectionately as the most ill-behaved little girl in America. It was, in fact, quite refreshing finally to be out of the limelight for a change. As far as Peter was concerned, Melinda was simply what she appeared to be—a highly respected teacher at a prestigious private academy. There was no need to tell him or anyone else, for that matter, that the young woman standing here in a designer sheath and elegant chignon was also the same pigtailed little demon who had once been voted by her elementary school principal as "the student most likely to end up in reform school."

Peter glanced at her curiously. "Is something the matter?"

"Not at all," Melinda replied hastily. "Shouldn't we be going?"

He gave a nod and held the door open. "The way I've planned it, we'll arrive just at the correct time. Not too early, and not too late."

"I see," Melinda mused vaguely, and reached for her cashmere coat. Peter Harrison was the most organized human being she had ever known. She thought of the endearing absent-mindedness of her father and the happy confusion that had always seemed to reign supreme in the Clarke family.

When they arrived, the fund-raising party to re-elect Congressman Sam Kendall was in full swing. Melinda glanced around the noisy living room of the colonial mansion with only mild interest. She had never cared much for politics and was not particularly impressed by the smattering of famous faces who mingled with the crowd.

"Isn't this terrific?" Peter practically gushed as he handed her a glass of imported champagne. "Besides the fact that he owns the local bank, is it any wonder that Ross Kendall is our most important client? Just look at all the VIPs he managed to pull in tonight to support his cousin!"

"Which one is Ross Kendall?" Melinda asked vaguely.

Peter squinted for a moment. "Hmm, I don't see him around, which isn't exactly a surprise. He really hates social events."

That makes two of us, Melinda said silently.

"Of course, he'll have to put in an appearance sometime, but— Look, there's the governor! And can you believe who's with him? That's Arthur Langley!"

"Who?" Melinda's heart sank. Please, let it be a mistake, she thought, panic-stricken.

"Arthur Langley, the great man himself!" Peter shook his head in amazement as the distinguished white-haired gentleman paused in the middle of a conversation with the governor. He gazed in Melinda's direction, one of his bushy eyebrows raised in puzzled recognition. Arthur Langley was considered to be America's greatest living elder statesman. The consummate diplomat had served eight presidents, and had been credited with helping avert political upheavals throughout the world. But right at this moment, the former ambassador was wondering what his goddaughter was doing at a dull fund-raiser.

"You're going to think I've flipped my lid," Peter whispered. "But Arthur Langley is looking at me as if he knows me!"

"Really?" Melinda murmured nervously.

"I'm sure I'm mistaken." The young man shrugged.

Just then, a society matron placed a heavily jeweled arm on the elderly diplomat's shoulder, successfully diverting his attention.

"I guess it must have been my imagination," Peter said, then sighed regretfully. "Just wishful thinking. Wouldn't it be great to know someone as important as Arthur Langley?"

"Would it mean that much to you?"

"Are you kidding? It would mean everything! With both my bosses, Caton *and* Henderson, here tonight? Do you have any idea how impressed they would be?"

Melinda felt suddenly in need of fresh air. The last person she wanted to be seen with right now was her Uncle Arthur, a man who took his own giant spotlight with him wherever he went. Coming to this party had been a big mistake.

"Listen, Peter," she said slowly. "I realize you have a bit of circulating to do, but would you mind if I stepped outside for a while?"

"I...I'd like you to meet some people," he protested.

"It's just getting a bit warm in here all of a sudden."

But Peter's eyes were already wandering across the room. "There's Mr. Caton, standing by himself. This is probably my only chance to talk to him alone tonight." He paused. "Would you mind very much if I—"

Melinda tried not to sound too relieved. "No, go right ahead."

"I'll try not to be very long." Peter planted a brief kiss on her cheek and strode purposefully toward the other side of the huge living room.

Without hesitating another moment, Melinda walked over to the French doors leading out onto the patio. There was a brisk chill in the night air, but she scarcely felt it on the bare skin of her shoulders. The champagne had given her a heady, heated flush. Standing on the far end of the deserted lawn, Melinda leaned against the stone balustrade. She was troubled and confused. Was it so wrong to wish to keep her life beyond Perryville private? Explaining her relationship with Arthur Langley to Peter would open up a giant can of worms. The great statesman had known Melinda's mother since she had been a struggling young journalist in Washington, D.C. Years later, in a festering jungle halfway around the world, Joanna Prescott had been responsible for rescuing Arthur Langley during a bizarre twist of fate. The courageous reporter had single-handedly delivered the diplomat from a terrifying hostage incident. But that was another story. The point was, that to reveal she was the daughter of the famous Joanna Prescott, was also to reveal her connection to the comic strip character Little Lindy. Melinda shook her head defiantly. "Forget it. I just won't do it!"

"You won't do what?" a deep voice inquired.

Startled, she whirled around to see a tall figure looming in the darkness. "I . . . I thought I was alone out here."

"So did I."

Melinda nervously set her empty champagne glass down on the balustrade. "The truth is, I think I prefer being outside."

"Join the club," the man's voice had a cynical edge. "What are you hiding from?"

She hesitated. It was so odd having such a conversation with a total stranger, yet there was something soothingly anonymous about the darkness. "Why would I be hiding?"

"You tell me."

Melinda sighed. "I hate politics and I hate parties."

"I agree it is a rather deadly combination." There was a hint of amusement in the man's tone.

"I never should have come," she confessed bluntly.

"Why did you, then?"

"I'm beginning to wonder, myself," Melinda mused. "Why did *you* come?"

There was a long pause. "Let's just say I'm here because of a long-standing obligation."

She smiled. "In other words, we'd both rather be someplace else."

"Undoubtedly." The man's face was still shrouded in shadow, until the next moment, when he lit a cigarette. In the brief, flickering light, Melinda could discern a sharp, angular face. "Although," he added unexpectedly, "I don't have any complaints about the present situation."

Melinda quirked an eyebrow. "Good heavens, is that a compliment?"

"Take it any way you like," came the bland response. "You're certainly more interesting to talk with than those brainless sycophants inside there."

"Gee, I suppose I ought to say thank you." She smiled in spite of herself.

"It's pitch dark, but I'm willing to bet you've got a smile on your face," her shadowy companion ventured.

"That's amazing." Melinda crossed her arms against the night chill. "Exactly how perceptive are you?"

"Well, let's see." He relaxed his tall frame against the balustrade, drawing a bit closer to Melinda in the process. "From your voice, I'd say you're well-educated, somewhere in your mid-twenties, and from the rustle of your dress I'd guess you're wearing silk."

"Uncanny."

"Would you care to hear more?"

"Please. This is fascinating." This was all rather unnerving in a tantalizingly unexpected way. Melinda found something strangely delightful about a conversation in the dark with this stranger.

"Hmm...you're also wearing pearls, probably two strands, from the sound they make as you clink them together between your fingers. Tell me, do women always fidget like that when they're nervous!"

"Not to discredit your impressive skills of deduction, sir," she commented wryly, "but there is a difference between being nervous and unnerved."

There was another pause. "Are you saying that I unnerve you?"

A delicious kind of tension hovered in the April night. If Melinda were honest with herself, she had never before enjoyed such a clever repartee before, not with Peter nor any other man. "Well," she conceded, "it is rather unsettling to have a perfect stranger be able to describe you without using his eyesight."

It was the man's turn to laugh. "Up until now, I've only used my sense of hearing. There are other senses as well."

"Really?"

"Of course. Let's not forget one's sense of smell." He took a step closer. "The perfume you're wearing, for example. It's fresh, light and distinctly unusual. I don't recall ever smelling a scent like that before. It's delightfully different yet very feminine."

"Is that another compliment?"

"Absolutely. Most perfumes that women wear these days are so heavy they knock you over like a steamroller."

"Thank you. In fact, this perfume was created especially for me."

"I'm impressed."

"Don't be. My father's a chemist. He came up with the formula as a sixteenth birthday gift. I can't tell you how much money it's saved him on presents all these years. I get a bottle every Christmas."

"Well, all I can say is my compliments to your father," her companion murmured softly, and drew even closer. "Let's see, what other senses can one utilize in this situation? Ah, yes, then there's touch!" He reached out a tentative finger to rest lightly on the bare skin of Melinda's shoulder.

Hastily she drew back. "That's quite all right. The first two senses were more than adequate!"

"Now I *know* I make you nervous," her companion observed with surprise. "You've got goose bumps!"

"Don't flatter yourself." Melinda tried to sound severe but failed. "I'm reacting to the weather, not *you,* Mr. X." What a fascinating voice this man had. Like deep velvet.

Again came that wonderful laugh. "'Mr. X!' That's a new one. I'll have to remember that. It seems I've been called everything else in the book."

"You have my sympathy."

"Honey, I'll bet your sympathy is really something to see."

"That's hardly a proper thing to say to a stranger," she said reprovingly.

"Is that what we are? Strangers?"

At once, Melinda was uncomfortable with the subtle turn the conversation had taken. "Of course we're strangers. We don't know each other from Adam."

The man seemed to consider this remark. "Odd, because I was just beginning to believe we know each other quite well."

She cleared her throat. "Well, you're wrong."

"Am I?"

"Certainly. I don't even know your name."

There was a long silence. "I don't know your name, either." He tossed his cigarette carelessly to the ground. "A situation that is easily remedied. Ladies first."

"Forget it."

"Very well, then. I'll go first." He hesitated briefly, "My name is—"

"No, wait," Melinda said suddenly. "Don't tell me."

"Why not?" He seemed somewhat taken aback.

She gave a sigh. "The truth is, I'd rather not know."

"Hmm, are you really that fainthearted?" There was an odd note in his voice.

Melinda reached out and touched his sleeve in a conciliatory gesture. "Sometimes it's better to remain anonymous, don't you agree, Mr. X?"

At her unexpected touch the man was absolutely still. "Sometimes, anonymity isn't the best idea." Even through the fine material of his jacket, he exuded an unmistakable strength.

"I disagree, Mr. X." Melinda tried to sound light. "I've always found that being anonymous has always been a better idea."

There was a perceptible pause. "Apparently you make a practice of it. I find that rather puzzling."

She laughed nervously. "It's nothing of the sort, believe me."

A firm hand suddenly stilled her own against his sleeve. "Now I'm curious. What would a young woman like yourself possibly have to be so secretive about?"

Melinda bit her lip involuntarily. "I'd better be getting back inside."

The man did not release his strong grasp. "Now you're trying to change the subject. That makes me even more curious. Which brings us back to the first question—what are you hiding from?"

"I already told you."

He reached for another cigarette. "Yes, I know. You don't care for parties or politics." His gaunt features flickered for the briefest moment in the glow of his metallic lighter. "Why do I have a feeling that it isn't the real answer?"

There was a mesmerizing quality to his words that actually made Melinda hesitate. "Does it matter?"

He took a thoughtful drag on the cigarette. "Yes, it does matter."

"Why?"

"Why? Because it makes life more interesting."

She pursed her mouth tightly. "Isn't your life interesting enough without delving nosily into other people's private affairs?"

"Mmm, now you've *really* whetted my curiosity!"

"That answers my question," Melinda scoffed. "If all this makes you so curious, you must lead a pretty dull life."

"I had no idea just *how* dull until this minute," the man agreed amiably.

"Oh, the truth is—" She threw her hands up in the air. "You just wouldn't understand."

"Try me."

"It's rather a long story."

"I've got plenty of time."

"Well, frankly, I don't." The night wind began to blow even more harshly through the trees shrouding the huge back lawn. The moonless sky seemed so desolate. Almost claustrophobic.

"You're in quite a hurry all of a sudden."

"I don't know if you've noticed, Mr. X, but it's getting rather chilly out here." Melinda wrapped her arms even more tightly around her slender frame.

At once, hands reached out in the darkness, and a man's jacket was settled gently around her bare shoulders. The brief brush of his fingers against her skin caused an involuntary shiver. "Is that better?"

"Yes." Melinda barely managed an audible response.

"So, you were about to tell me a long story."

Who was this man anyhow? How on earth did he manage to evoke such a confusing reaction in her? Melinda wondered. Part of her wanted to stay and tell this virtual stranger everything. Another part of her couldn't wait to flee the darkened patio and return to the bright hazard that awaited in the crowded living room. It was all rather bewildering, to say the least.

"Look," she uttered finally, "I shouldn't even be here."

"What does that mean?" he probed. "You shouldn't be out here on the terrace or you shouldn't be here at this little soiree?"

"Both." She pursed her mouth tightly. "I shouldn't be here at all."

"You were about to explain *why.*"

"No, I wasn't."

He ignored her. "Of course, you were. Now, let's see what it could be. You shouldn't be here because you're not on the guest list?" He gave a brief laugh. "No, that's not very believable. I mean, who in his right mind would want to crash one of these deadly parties?"

"I agree."

"Ah, I think I know! You shouldn't be here because you're incognito and you're afraid you'll be recognized!" He waited a moment for Melinda's blithe retort, but there wasn't one. After a distinct pause, the man said in a slightly different tone, "Is that it?"

"Excuse me?"

"I know your voice too well by now for any prevarication. So, that's it," he mused. "You're afraid someone inside there knows you from someplace else."

It was useless to deny anything, Melinda conceded with mild panic. There was no point in arguing with this astonishingly perceptive individual.

"Of course—" the man edged closer "—I'm not ordinarily a very inquisitive person...."

"Oh, *sure!*"

"But I find myself extremely intrigued by your predicament."

"You're just plain nosy."

"The truth is," he said, "I can't help but wonder about you. Obviously there's someone at this party you'd prefer to avoid. Might I presume it is an amorous ex-boyfriend?"

"Please!" Melinda pulled off the fine wool jacket with mild indignance and pressed it blindly into her companion's arms. "Take back your coat, Mr. X. Thank you very much, and good *night!*"

But before she could pull away, a firm hand grasped her wrist. "Coward," came the gentle taunt. "Why can't you tell the truth? We all have people in our lives we'd rather not see again."

"That isn't it at all."

"No?"

"*No.* The fact is, it's all rather complicated. Meanwhile, it's time I was getting back inside. My . . . my date will be wondering what happened to me."

"Your date. Who is he?"

"Does it matter?"

There was a pause. "No, not really." Taut fingers caressed Melinda's wrist lightly. Almost a phantom touch. But before she could even react to this unexpected intimacy, the man's hand dropped abruptly to his side. "If I were your date, I wouldn't let you wander unescorted onto a darkened terrace."

Melinda felt a flush in her cheeks. "Well, you're not my date."

"Obviously." The cynicism had returned to his voice. "I'd say this gentleman friend of yours is either woefully inattentive or just plain careless."

"*I'd* say it's time to return inside."

The tall stranger seemed to consider this. "You're quite right, of course. We can't hide out here forever."

"No, we can't." Melinda tried to sound matter-of-fact.

"After all, grown-ups aren't supposed to play hooky, and we both have our responsibilities in there, as dull as they may be."

"You're absolutely right," she agreed.

With a resigned sigh, the man discarded his second cigarette onto the stone floor and ground it beneath his shoe. "Of course, you realize that if the two of us walk back inside together, people might talk."

"That had occurred to me, yes."

"Not that I give a damn what people think, you understand...but it might be best if you went in a few minutes before I did. It is, after all, a small town and tongues do tend to wag."

"I couldn't agree more." Melinda hesitated. The two of them both seemed to be waiting for the other to say something. Perhaps it was her imagination. "Well, good night, Mr. X."

"Good night, Miss X." There was an odd note in his voice. "I've decided that you're quite right about this anonymity business. It does have its advantages."

"I'm glad you feel that way," Melinda murmured, strangely disappointed for reasons she couldn't even fathom. It was all somewhat of a letdown. In another moment, she would walk away from this man, past the tall row of hedges that kept the terrace in total darkness. Once inside the tall French doors, there was no way she would ever recognize this curious stranger.

"Go ahead," he said quietly. "Walk away and don't look back."

Chapter Two

When Melinda returned to the crowded, noisy living room it took several moments to reaccustom her eyes to the bright lights.

"There you are!" exclaimed a familiar voice behind her. "I hope you weren't too bored while I was gone." Peter smiled sheepishly and handed her another glass of champagne.

"Bored?" Melinda echoed vaguely.

He glanced around deprecatingly at the other guests. "There are mostly old fogies here."

"Oh? I hadn't noticed."

"Don't try to make me feel better." Her date sighed guiltily. "Leaving you here to fend for yourself while I trotted off to talk to the boss. Of course you must have been bored to pieces."

Melinda shrugged. "Forget it. I wasn't bored at all." Almost absentmindedly, she found herself

scanning the large, colonial-style living room. Somewhere amongst all these unfamiliar faces was the man
from the terrace. Melinda couldn't help but wonder
who he was and what he looked like. It wasn't that
she was interested in him as a *man,* she told herself
quickly. No, that wasn't it at all. She was just a little
bit curious, that's all. How often did one get the opportunity to have an intriguing conversation in the
dark?

"...So isn't that terrific news?" Peter was saying.

"Excuse me?" Melinda snapped back to reality.

"Haven't you been listening?" Peter appeared
slightly bewildered. "I was telling you that Mr.
Caton—he's the senior partner—is very impressed
with the work I've been doing for Ross Kendall."

"That's great, Peter," she answered sincerely.

"It's better than great," he declared. "It's fantas-
tic! I mean," he began, his voice lowering, "just take
a look around you. The paintings on the wall, all this
antique furniture. Why, I heard that the crystal
chandelier up there is nearly two hundred years old.
It's supposed to have belonged to Thomas Jefferson,
can you believe it?"

"That's pretty impressive," she admitted.

"I mean, is it any wonder that the Kendalls are the
most important family in the county? Or that Ross
Kendall in particular is our most important client?"

On the other side of the room, Congressman Sam
Kendall, a balding, middle-aged man with a tired
smile, was still shaking hands and patiently listening
to the endless prattle of numerous fawning constitu-
ents. Melinda shook her head, completely mystified.
If she lived to be one hundred, she would never be

able to fathom the fascination politics held for so many people. Her own mother, once a member of the Washington press corps, had always viewed politicians with mild amusement. And then, of course, there was Uncle Arthur, who always made a point of insisting he was a diplomat, never a politician. It was especially through him that Melinda had learned never to be in awe of anyone, no matter how famous or influential.

Uncle Arthur. Somewhat belatedly, she was filled with remorse for not yet having greeted her beloved guardian. Purposefully, her eyes searched the vast living room once again. At last, Melinda spotted him leaning comfortably against one of the mahogany bookcases, his usual glass of soda water in his hand. Apparently he was engaged in an amusing conversation. At that precise moment, he threw back his head and roared with laughter. Fine, she decided, now was as good a time as any to stroll over and say hello.

Melinda set her glass down on one of the silver trays and said softly to Peter, "Excuse me for a minute."

He looked at her questioningly. "Where are you going?"

"I'll be right back." She touched him on his arm with gentle reassurance. "Don't go anywhere...." she said. "There's someone I'd like *you* to meet."

"I didn't think you knew anybody at this party," Peter remarked curiously.

"I didn't think so, either." Leaving her handsome date with his mouth full of hot crab canapés, Melinda strode across the room. Arthur Langley and his unidentified companion were still in the midst of laughter. There was nothing like the deep, rich sound of hearty male laughter, Melinda thought. It reminded her of the holidays, and of her three brothers, now fully grown, coming home at Christmastime.

The distinguished diplomat paused in midsentence, and his thin lips broadened into a delighted smile. "Lindy!"

"Hi, Uncle Arthur," Melinda said as she embraced him affectionately.

"And here I thought these old eyes had been playing tricks on me, when I saw you before." The old man shook his head. "What on earth brings you to this little wingding? I thought you avoided politic affairs like the plague, darling."

She grinned sheepishly. "It's a favor to the person I'm dating."

"I figured it was something like that." Arthur Langley chuckled, and keeping an arm around her waist turned to his companion. "My goddaughter prefers root canal surgery to politics."

"Really," remarked an astonishingly familiar voice.

Startled, Melinda glanced at the other man for the first time. He was tall, well-dressed with dark hair and gaunt, angular features. Right now, his brown eyes were staring at her in a rather penetrating manner. So this was the enigmatic stranger she had encountered on the patio. Was it possible that he recognized her? Melinda wondered uncomfortably.

"Absolutely. I believe the last occasion we managed to drag this dear child to was that White House dinner for that charming British princess who insisted on meeting the famous Little Li—"

"Yes, well—" She cleared her throat quickly. "Time certainly does fly."

"I understand from your mother that you're teaching at the Perryvile Academy, and that—" he stopped himself. "Now, where on earth are my manners? Lindy, dear, I'd like you to meet our host for the evening, Ross Kendall. Ross, this lovely child is my goddaughter, Melinda Clarke."

"How do you do, Miss Clarke." A hard hand clasped hers briefly. "Is it possible that we've met before?"

"I don't think so," Melinda stammered. How utterly mortifying. Ross Kendall, of all people! Why did these crazy things keep happening to her?

"I only ask because there's something familiar about you." He paused. "Your voice."

For the first time in her life, Melinda was actually tongue-tied. It was more than just the embarrassing coincidence. Talking with a mysterious stranger in the dark was one thing, but actually meeting him face-to-face was another matter altogether. Ross Kendall was not a handsome man by any means. One side of his face, from the eyebrow down past the jawline, was marred by a network of jagged scars. Nonetheless, there was a vital strength that seemed to radiate from him. He was so undeniably, disturbingly *male*. "What about my voice?" Melinda inquired in a deliberately different tone.

He regarded her intently. "Forget it. Perhaps it was my imagination." There was a cynical twist to his lips. "However, allow me to compliment you on your perfume."

She flushed bright pink. He knew. He'd known the moment she had walked across the room. "Uh, thank you." Lord, she felt like a total idiot.

Arthur Langley, the eternal diplomat, observed this little exchange with a mixture of curiosity and puzzlement. His sharp eyes moved back and forth between his two companions as if he were watching some kind of tennis match.

"So," Ross Kendall murmured quietly. "Tell me more about your charming goddaughter, Arthur."

The older man beamed. "As you can see, I'm very proud of her. In many ways, Melinda is very much like her mother—you've heard of *her,* of course—the absolutely incredible Joanna Prescott."

There was a significant pause. "Your mother is *the* Joanna Prescott?"

"The one and only." Arthur Langley practically sounded like some kind of proud parent.

"Melinda." Ross Kendall seemed to be working it out in his mind. "And Arthur called you Lindy just before..."

Oh, no. Here it comes, Melinda thought with a shudder.

"So that would make you—" he quirked an astonished eyebrow "—Little Lindy? *You're* Little Lindy?"

"Amazing, isn't it?" Arthur Langley grinned.

"Amazing." There was an odd note in the other man's voice. "All these years, I've always wondered what the real Lindy must be like. And now, here she is in the flesh."

The way he continued to stare made Melinda feel downright jittery. If she'd still been holding that champagne glass, she more than likely would have crushed the fragile stem.

She met his glance evenly and said, "As someone remarked to me earlier this evening—it's a very small town, and tongues do tend to wag."

In the brief silence that followed, the man who had been the stranger on the terrace accepted the acknowledgement. There would be no more pretending that the conversation in the darkness had never taken place. "Yes," Ross Kendall concurred, "it *is* a very small town."

"...So I'd appreciate it if you kept the 'Lindy' thing to yourself."

"For heaven's sake, *why?*" Arthur Langley interjected in bewilderment.

"You know very well I've been trying to live it down for years, Uncle Arthur."

"Do you mean to say that nobody else in Perryville has any idea who you really are?"

Melinda turned back to the man who had just spoken those disbelieving words. "That's correct, Mr. Kendall, and I'd prefer to keep it that way. I have a reputation to maintain."

"Oh, yes," came the dry observation. "You're a teacher at the academy. Hmm, so the worst-behaved little girl in the world actually became a *teacher*. I suppose that's what is known as poetic justice."

She cleared her throat uncomfortably. "Uncle Arthur, if you happen to have a moment, there's someone I'd like you to meet."

"Ah, yes! You must mean your young man." Arthur Langley nodded with pleasure.

"He...he isn't exactly 'my young man,'" Melinda felt strangely compelled to explain. "He's my...my—" She searched for the word to explain her relationship with Peter Harrison.

"Your *date.*" Ross Kendall finished for her.

She could actually see his lips twitch in amusement. "Anyway, he'd very much like to meet you, Uncle Arthur."

"Why certainly, I'd be delighted. Where is this paragon?"

Melinda hesitated. "There's just one thing. He's kind of a straight arrow. He doesn't know about Little Lindy."

"Hmm. When were you planning on telling him?"

"Not right now." She looked at the older man beseechingly. "Please, Uncle Arthur. Promise you won't say anything."

He kissed her cheek lightly. "My lips are sealed." He turned to Ross Kendall, who now stood strangely silent. "Excuse us for a moment, won't you, Ross?"

"Certainly."

Melinda extended her hand mechanically. "A pleasure meeting you, Mr. Kendall."

"The feeling is definitely mutual," he uttered quietly, "And the name is *Ross.*"

"Ross," Melinda conceded, and waited for the hard, tanned hand to release its grasp.

"By the way," came the soft murmur, "silk and pearls can be a devastating combination in the light of day." Abruptly he released her hand and walked away.

Arthur Langley gazed curiously at his godchild's flushed face. "A rather interesting fellow, wouldn't you say, my dear?"

"Who?"

"What do you mean, *who?* Ross Kendall, of course!"

Melinda shrugged. "I suppose so."

"That's not very enthusiastic," he said, his eyes twinkling. "Now, where is this young man you wanted me to meet?"

With no small measure of disbelief, Peter Harrison watched Melinda walking toward him with the distinguished diplomat in tow. Self-consciously, he gulped down the remainder of a cocktail sausage and prayed there wasn't any mustard on the front of his shirt. Melinda was smiling faintly at him, and *what* exactly was she saying?

"Uncle Arthur, I'd like you to meet Peter Harrison, a good friend of mine."

"Delighted to meet you, young man." The world-famous statesman shook his hand heartily.

"Uh, it's an honor, sir...." he managed to stammer. *Uncle* Arthur? He gaped at Melinda stupefied. "Arthur Langley is your *uncle?*"

"Not exactly," she explained.

"I'm a very old friend of the family." Arthur Langley paused. "Melinda's parents had the incredible wisdom and foresight to name me her godfather."

"She... she never told me." Peter sounded almost peevish.

"It never came up in the conversation." Melinda shrugged. For some odd reason, she found the handsome attorney's attitude slightly annoying.

"Don't try to understand the female mind, Peter." The aging diplomat waved his hand expansively. "But if you take my advice, you'll find that most women prefer being a little mysterious. Inevitably it adds to their allure." He seemed almost to be testing the other man.

"Yes, of course, you're absolutely right," her date agreed hastily.

Melinda stared at him, mystified. She had never seen Peter so flustered. "Uncle Arthur, did I happen to mention that Peter is an associate at the firm of Caton and Henderson?"

"I'm about to become a junior partner, in fact," the young lawyer added, and winked at Melinda. "I was going to break the good news to you a little later."

"How wonderful!" she exclaimed. "That's great news, Peter!" Impulsively Melinda embraced him.

He actually blushed. "Gee, I ought to get promoted more often!"

"Congratulations," Arthur Langley said, patting him on the back enthusiastically.

"Uh, thank you, sir." Peter Harrison was completely overcome.

It was rumored that the sharpest eyesight in the world belonged to Arthur Langley. While this might have been an exaggeration, it was an undeniable fact that the renowned former ambassador reached his celebrated status in the field of foreign diplomacy by never permitting the slightest, most minute detail to escape his scrutiny. And far across the room, he couldn't fail to notice the taut expression on Ross Kendall's gaunt face. Even sixty feet away, it was impossible not to see the man's jaw tighten perceptibly at the exact moment Melinda had so happily embraced young Harrison. And because Arthur Langley sincerely believed his own legend as the world's foremost negotiator of great alliances, he decided to help nature along. Well, maybe just *prod* it a little bit. Young people were so stubborn these days. They never knew what was best for them. At least, not at first. *A diplomat was never off duty,* he thought, smiling a secret inner-smile. He cleared his throat. "Won't you excuse us, my dear?" he asked of Melinda. "I'd like to get to know this young man a little better." He gestured toward the bar. "Tell me some more about your work at Caton and Henderson, Peter," Arthur Langley entreated in his most fatherly manner. "Now what type of law do you specialize in?"

Peter was completely beside himself. "Oh, you wouldn't find it very interesting, sir...."

"Nonsense, I'm sure it's absolutely fascinating. Tell me all about it as we walk over to the bar. I need another soda water. And I believe your glass is empty, too."

The next moment, Melinda was standing in the middle of the room, staring after them in disbelief. What kind of game was Uncle Arthur playing? Since when had he ever cared about the career aspirations of a small-town lawyer? It was all very bewildering.

"So, that was your date," a deep voice said behind her.

"Yes—" Melinda turned around and met that now-familiar, piercing brown stare. "As a matter of fact."

"Despite your denials to the contrary, the two of you seem to be pretty...close."

"And what is *that* supposed to mean?"

Ross Kendall glanced down into his half-empty glass of Scotch. "Never mind, it's none of my business, anyway."

"That's right, it isn't."

He shrugged. "I assume you know that Harrison is one of my attorneys."

"Yes." It was suddenly very hot in the crowded living room. Melinda brushed a stray blond wisp away from her heated forehead. "Peter mentioned it this evening."

The dark eyes traveled appreciatively down the gentle curves of her slender figure. "Then you're aware of my position in this town."

"I beg your pardon?"

In an almost awkward gesture, he dug one hand into the pocket of his expensive dark dress slacks. "My position as the most successful banker in the county, Miss Clarke."

"Why are you telling me this?"

Ross Kendall's tone was cynical. "I thought you might find such information...interesting."

Melinda crossed her arms. "Really. And what makes you think I'd be particularly interested in your résumé, Mr. Kendall?"

"In my case, it seems to make a difference with most women."

"I don't understand."

His eyes lingered briefly on the creamy skin above the low-cut silk bodice. "Of course, you do. You're the daughter of an internationally acclaimed journalist, and the godchild of a living legend, not to mention the fact that you're a household name, yourself. You've moved in circles so high that they're out of the reach of most ordinary people."

"I thought we agreed not to talk about my... background."

"Arthur agreed. I never said a word." He paused. "Lindy Prescott Clarke, more than anyone else, you should recognize the difference that power and wealth make when selecting one's... friends."

She frowned. "Baloney, Mr. Kendall."

"Ross," he prompted. "And I daresay you're not being completely truthful."

"And *I* daresay you haven't the slightest idea of what you're talking about."

"Don't I?" The lanky banker shot a dark glance in the direction of the bar, where Peter was regaling a sleepy-eyed Arthur Langley with his entire life story. "Your boyfriend over there looks more like a California surfer than a lawyer for the stuffiest firm in the state."

"He's not my boyfriend... exactly."

"Then what is he, *exactly?*" Ross Kendall was almost scathing. "You certainly hugged him like he was your 'one and only.'"

"I thought we had agreed that it was none of your business."

He regarded her solemnly. "I didn't mean for us to argue. I merely wanted to point out the obvious."

"The obvious *what?*"

"Quite simply, that as the owner of three banks, a historical mansion, not to mention numerous other holdings, I have substantially more to offer than a mere junior partner in a small-town law firm."

Melinda stared at him as if she hadn't heard him correctly. "What are you saying?"

His lips tightened. "I think you know exactly what I'm saying."

She felt the blood suddenly rush to her head. "Are you making a pass, Mr. Kendall?"

"Absolutely."

"And are you always this . . . blunt?"

"Was I being blunt?" He reached over and ran a finger lightly across her flushed cheek, causing a tingle straight down to Melinda's toes. "I thought that I was simply stating the facts."

"I don't recall ever asking." Her voice actually shook.

"Yes." He nodded dryly and pulled his hand back. "I know. You were far too preoccupied with lover-boy over there. Your boyfriend is considered to be the handsomest fellow in town. My female tellers have been known to swoon whenever he comes into the bank." His tone was tinged with mild sarcasm.

"How many times do I have to tell you?" She rolled her eyes in exasperation. "He isn't my boy-friend!"

"I think the lady doth protest too much."

"Fine. Think whatever you want!"

"I'd rather not waste time playing games, Melinda." There was an odd glimmer in his eyes. "I'd rather be spending the time more . . . interestingly."

Was he actually trying to seduce her? Melinda thought in utter disbelief. The man barely knew her, yet here he was, expertly, confidently, trying to draw her into his masculine web. Who did Mr. Ross Kendall think he was, anyhow? Of all the absolute, unmitigated nerve! Trying to impress *her* with his money and position, as if she were some kind of brainless, superficial bimbo! Coldly Melinda drew herself up to her full height of five foot four. "Do you know the meaning of the word *chutzpah,* Mr. Kendall?"

"Why?"

"Because it describes your utter gall, your sheer *nerve,* better than any other word I can think of—that's why."

He seemed almost amused. "Really."

She shook her head. "You are without a doubt, the most arrogant, egotistical man it has ever been my misfortune to encounter."

"Now, wait a minute—"

"In addition, Mr. Kendall, you are an appallingly bad judge of character. *Good night!*"

Without another word, Melinda turned and strode quickly to the other side of the huge, noisy living room, leaving Ross Kendall standing alone with a stunned expression on his hard face.

Chapter Three

Arthur Langley managed to spend a few moments alone with his goddaughter before the evening was over. "I couldn't help noticing how well you and Ross seemed to be getting along, my dear."

Melinda almost choked on the words. "You actually thought the two of us were getting along?"

The elderly statesman regarded her curiously. "Suffice it to say, you've made quite a conquest."

"I don't think so, Uncle Arthur."

"Oh, I'd stake my professional reputation on it." He gave an approving nod. "Frankly I'm quite pleased. I've known Ross Kendall for the past ten years, and I can assure you, he is a man of substance—"

"Yes, well," she interrupted hastily. "I don't happen to be even remotely interested in Mr. Kendall."

"Hmm," came the dubious reply.

"It's true, Uncle Arthur. The man and I have absolutely nothing in common, not to mention the fact that he is an egotistical, smug, self-satisfied male chauvinist—"

The silver-haired diplomat's eyes danced. "Fascinating! Do tell me more about how uninterested you are in the man! I'm all ears, my dear."

Melinda gave him a chastening look. "And anyway, the man I happen to be interested in is Peter Harrison, in case you've forgotten."

He shrugged. "Ah, yes. Peter."

She gave a bright smile. "I think he's terribly attractive, don't you?"

"A veritable Adonis."

Melinda looked at him hopefully. "Didn't you find him extremely intelligent?"

"Yes, very intelligent," he said, then paused. "And do you know who else is remarkably bright? Ross Kendall."

"Uncle, we were talking about *Peter.* So, you spent quite some time talking together. Don't you think he's simply terrific?"

Arthur Langley's expression remained bland. "The important thing is that *you* like him, Lindy."

Melinda's heart sank. *The important thing is that you like him.* That line was the ultimate "kiss of death" when delivered by parents, relatives or friends. What it generally meant when translated was "Thumbs down. We're not impressed."

As far as Peter Harrison was concerned, it had been the most gratifying evening of his entire life. He had not failed to notice the envious glances when he'd ar-

rived at the Kendall fund-raiser with a stunning young
woman on his arm, and when he had finally intro-
duced Melinda to the senior partners, they had both
smiled at him approvingly. It had been most gratifying, indeed. But by far, the highlight of the evening
came when Arthur Langley took him in tow and engaged him in a private conversation for over half an
hour. By the end of the party, the two of them were
old friends. Well, old acquaintances, at least, Peter
corrected himself. This, too, had not gone unnoticed
by the senior partners, Peter realized with a full heart.
It was obvious his stock had gone up at least ten
points at the venerated old firm of Caton and Henderson.

The only thing that puzzled him was Melinda's silence during the drive home. She had seemed
strangely subdued, or maybe it was just his imagination.

"You and I were the hit of the evening," he said,
beaming happily as they drove down the winding
private road that led away from the landmark Kendall estate.

"What?" Melinda had murmured distractedly.

Peter preened his stylishly cut blond hair in the
lighted rearview mirror. "Did you notice how the
waters parted when we walked across the room with
Arthur Langley?" He gave a sigh. "Man, I wish I'd
had a camera! Just to have taken a picture of the
looks on some of those old geezers' faces! I can't believe you're in so tight with the great Arthur Langley
and never breathed a word about it."

Melinda was staring out the passenger window at
the darkened landscape. Perryville was still a rela-

tively rural area, and the dense woods that bordered the road seemed almost ominous in the midnight gloom. "Excuse me?" she asked belatedly.

"I was wondering why you never mentioned your relationship with Arthur Langley before."

Melinda shrugged. "It's not something I go around talking about all the time. I've known him my whole life, so it's not a big deal to me."

"Well, if he were *my* godfather, I'd be bragging about it all the time."

But Melinda wasn't really paying much attention. She was too busy replaying that disturbing conversation with Ross Kendall over and over again in her mind. No man she had met before had ever affected her so viscerally. And even though there was a definite chill in the country night air, Melinda could still feel a hot flush suffuse her cheeks and the back of her neck. What was it Ross had said? *I'd rather not waste time playing games, Melinda.* Thus spoke the quintessential businessman, she thought cynically. What was it with some men that made them approach even the most personal aspects of their lives as if it were some kind of corporate takeover?

"Anyhow, so what were you talking to Ross Kendall about?"

"Nothing!" she said just a bit too loudly.

Peter shook his head with a knowing grin. "I'll bet you two were talking about me, right? Didn't I tell you he's pleased with my work? This last thing, especially. He's signed over some property to his daughter."

"His daughter?" It was strange to even picture that man having a child of his own. Melinda couldn't help but wonder what kind of father Ross Kendall would make.

"Apparently, the kid's been living overseas with her mother for years, but now she's back in Perryville."

"He's married?" Melinda found herself asking.

"Divorced." Her companion grinned broadly. "What a scandal *that* was! Almost seven years ago, and everyone in town still remembers it. According to rumor, she cleaned out the bank account and ran off with the tennis pro from the Perryville Country Club."

Melinda was oddly silent. For the first time, she felt just a little sorry for the blunt-spoken banker.

"So, what do you say?"

She looked over at Peter. "About what?"

"Our date on Saturday. I thought we might catch that new Wendell Wynberg film at the Greenfield Cinema."

"Sounds fine," Melinda murmured distractedly. Sure, why not? It wasn't as if she had any other plans, and Peter was a pleasant companion. True, he was not a particularly affectionate person. In fact, during the three weeks they had been dating, he had never tried to do anything more than kiss her goodnight. Not that there was anything wrong with that, she decided firmly. He was merely being a gentleman. And beside, it made life all the more uncomplicated. At almost twenty-five, Melinda had never yet had an intimate relationship with any man. This was not something she felt comfortable discussing with anyone, not even her closest girlfriends. But she did know that Arthur Langley's own daughter Liz had actually waited until she was married. The two of them were the same age and had gone to the same college in Washington, D.C. Because they had known each other as children, Liz often confided in Melinda.

"Wait until you meet a guy who makes your pulse race, Lindy," she had told her on the day of her wedding.

Well, so far that hadn't been a problem, Melinda thought. Peter Harrison still failed to make her pulse race, but why ask for the moon? And suddenly, her thoughts were invaded by the image of Ross Kendall. In just one evening's encounter, that man had managed to turn her complacent, serene little life upside down. How could someone she barely knew make her feel so...so unbalanced? So jittery? And he wasn't her type at all. He was far too bossy. Far too opinionated. Far too *everything*. It was a bitter pill to swallow, but like it or not, the arrogant Mr. Kendall had managed to get under her skin.

Replaying the events of the previous evening in his mind, Ross Kendall was at a loss to comprehend exactly where he had gone wrong. "Arrogant" and "egotistical" were the words she had used to describe him. He shook his head in bewilderment. Both descriptions were wholly inaccurate, Ross maintained firmly as he observed his haggard reflection in the mirror. No, *practical* was the word that came most quickly to mind. Another was *realistic*. He rinsed away the remaining shaving cream and regarded his face critically. He had never been a particularly attractive man, even before the accident, that much was true. But now, matters were even worse. What was it his ex-wife had said once? That he was "hard to look at?" Oh, yes, Ross thought bitterly, Deirdre had made her revulsion quite clear, but there was no doubting the truth behind her words. The scars from the crash had left him permanently disfigured, but he had learned how to compensate for his shortcomings. All too well. If he couldn't compete in the looks department, there were other ways for a man to ultimately achieve his objectives. *That,* Ross had most certainly learned from sour experience.

After Deirdre had left him, the women who came afterward had been quite willing to overlook his physical flaws in exchange for the rather obvious benefits that went along with carrying on a social relationship with a man of such wealth and influence. He had come to take it somewhat for granted that the entire female sex was of the same basic view. And so, last night, Ross had simply been expressing his desires in the most honest, direct way he knew how. He had absolutely no idea that Melinda Clarke would be so outright offended.

Melinda. Even thinking about her now, he felt his body actually tense. In the darkness of his terrace, he had been intrigued by a voice, an alluring scent and a touch of soft skin. As the two of them talked in the shadows, Ross had found himself wildly imagining what his companion looked like. When she left the patio without revealing her identity, he hadn't worried about finding her again. Confidently, Ross had no doubts he would recognize "Miss X" in an instant. There were very few young women at the reception. All he needed to search for were a double

strand of pearls and an extremely distinctive perfume. He expected the woman would be attractive,
but he never expected what finally came walking toward him as he stood chatting with Arthur Langley.
He hadn't asked for heaven. Melinda was lovely, far
lovelier than anyone he had seen in a very long time.
In fact, it had taken every bit of his iron self-control
not to say the poetic, boyish, utterly stupid things that
trembled on the tip of his tongue. He had taken just
one look at her beautifully expressive eyes and was
enchanted. The bright lights dancing over her golden
hair and creamy skin added even greater potency to
the delicious spell she had already cast over him. But
Ross's foolish bubble had burst the moment he wit-
nessed Melinda embracing Peter Harrison. They
made such a devastatingly picture-perfect young
couple. Just like the romantic ingenues in those glossy
magazine advertisements for imported champagne.
Ross felt a thud in his stomach.

Damn Peter Harrison and his all-American boy
good looks. Ross had never given much thought to
the young man before. He had considered him an
adequate attorney who could be trusted with bank
business. Other than that, Ross found him rather
unexceptional. But now, all he could think of was the
different ways he could eliminate his competition. In
business, he could have destroyed Peter Harrison with
a wave of his hand, but this wasn't business. Melinda
had made that startlingly clear.

Ross realized how he had been deluding himself. In
the dark anonymity of the stone terrace, he could
have held his own against anyone. Under the protec-
tive cloak of night, he could pretend that he was as

handsome and debonair as any matinee idol, with his facial features perfect and unmarred by disaster. In fact, for just a few brief moments on the terrace, Ross had actually managed to forget about the wounds that would never heal. Instead, he had deliciously savored his role as the mysterious "Mr. X." He had felt dashing and sophisticated for the first time in his life. But back in the real world, under the merciless glare of the bright lights reflecting from the ornate crystal chandelier, he knew it had all been an illusion. He would never be handsome or debonair. He would never be anything but what he really was—an unattractive man who had to pay for his feminine companionship. And even though he wanted to possess Melinda Clarke, with a raw urgency that startled him, Ross now understood that it was inevitably a lost cause. Hadn't she made it quite clear that she disliked him intensely? That she preferred handsome, struggling young attorneys to rich, established but ugly bankers?

Angrily Ross slammed the door of the medicine cabinet and found himself once again face-to-face with his unattractive reflection. The subject was now closed. Never before had any female made him feel so absolutely vulnerable. So completely powerless. He was up against a stone wall, unable to break through and take what he wanted. And what he wanted was Melinda. But she was the one woman his money could not buy.

Ross's black mood continued all through breakfast. He scowled when Willis, the butler who had served the family faithfully for twenty-five years, merely inquired if he wished to have more coffee. Then, when Miriam, the plump, good-natured housekeeper and cook cheerfully informed him that last night's party had been an unqualified success, he murmured something unintelligible under his breath. The two employees exchanged baffled glances and returned hastily to the safety of the kitchen.

"Are you mad at me, Daddy?" a small voice finally spoke up.

Startled, Ross set down his morning paper. He stared at his young daughter. "Mad at you? Of course not, pumpkin."

"You *look* mad."

"I'm not mad!"

"Then why are you yelling, Daddy?"

That plaintive observation stopped him dead in his tracks. Rarely, if at all, had he ever raised his voice to his only child. He regarded Jenny silently. At ten, she was small for her age, with solemn brown eyes very much like his own. But she had spent the past seven years living in England with her mother. Getting to know each other again was going to take a good deal of time, Ross realized. The truth was, he and his young daughter were virtual strangers. After the divorce, he had sincerely believed he had done the right thing by giving up custody to Deirdre. He had belonged to the old-fashioned school that believed a child needed to be with its mother. Besides, there had been many long, grueling months of recovery after the accident. Back then, he had been made painfully aware that during that time, he would be unable to give his child the love and attention she required. But now, things were different, and Ross fully intended to make up for lost time.

Now he leaned across the table and affectionately touched Jenny's shoulder. "What would you like to do today?"

The little girl stared at him. "Daddy, it's Thursday!"

"So?"

She shook her head. "It's a school day."

"Oh, right." He hesitated. "How do you like your new school?"

There was a silence. "It's okay."

Ross sighed. "I know it's not your school in London."

"No, it isn't."

"The Perryville Academy is where your aunts and your cousins, and even your grandmother went, honey."

"The kids all make fun of me," came the dull reply.

Ross looked at her in surprise. "You're a *Kendall.* Why would anyone make fun of you?"

"Everybody says I talk weird."

His mouth tightened. "You have an English accent, that's all."

"In London, they said I had an American accent."

"Believe me, Jenny. After the other kids get to know you, they'll stop teasing and you'll all become friends."

"Really?"

"Trust me."

"Were all those people at the house last night *your* friends?"

Ross gave a tired smile. "Not exactly." No, most of them were certainly not friends of *his*. Except, perhaps, for his cousin Sam and, of course, Arthur Langley. Then there was also the matter of Melinda Clarke. Suddenly, out of the blue, a thought occurred to him. "Tell me, pumpkin. Who's your English teacher at school?"

Jenny rolled her eyes. "I *hate* her."

He was startled. "Is she really so awful?"

"She's boring, and she has teacher's pets."

Ross tried to sound casual. "What's your teacher's name again? Miss . . . Clarke?"

His daughter stared back at him. "No, it's Miss Monroe. Gee, I only *wish* I had Miss Clarke!"

"You do?"

"She's the nicest teacher in the whole school."

"Is that so?"

"Yes, but she doesn't teach fourth grade. Just the older girls."

"That's too bad." Well, he thought ironically, it would seem he was not the only Kendall who was being denied the company of the elusive Miss Melinda Clarke.

Ross had no idea that fate was about to change that situation completely.

Chapter Four

Melinda was finding it almost impossible to concentrate that day. For the first time since her arrival at the Perryville Academy, she found her mind wandering during class. While giving a lecture on the fundamentals of creative writing, she kept daydreaming about a tall stranger on a darkened terrace. The stranger was lighting a cigarette and talking about her perfume. This image was so distracting that once or twice Melinda's voice actually drifted off in the middle of a sentence, and her students started to look at one another in amusement.

"It sounds like you've got spring fever, Miss Clarke," giggled Lonnie Ellison. The redheaded teenager was captain of the basketball team and president of the senior class.

Melinda folded her arms and attempted to look stern. "Spring fever, indeed!"

"Gosh, Miss Clarke." Brenda Matthews grinned through a mouthful of silver braces. "What else would you call it when a teacher stops talking and just stares off into space?"

"It's called collecting one's thoughts, Brenda."

"I'm *so* sure." The only daughter of Harlan Matthews, the California real-estate tycoon, was completely unconvinced.

"Thank you so much for sharing *that* special thought with us, Brenda." Melinda tried to sound severe and failed. The entire class was smiling back at her, knowingly. She gave a sigh. Had she forgotten so quickly what it had been like to be a teenager? Melinda recalled how nearly impossible it had been for an adult to try and pull the wool over *her* eyes when she was a wise and all-knowing seventeen-year-old. Good grief, she must be getting old!

Melinda cleared her throat uncomfortably. "Very well, class. Call it 'spring fever' or just a reverie—but tomorrow, we will discuss how such momentary lapses are often the basis of great creative thought."

As if on cue, another stray image descended upon Melinda uninvited. The picture of glimmering brown eyes and a devastatingly masculine profile. *Drat you, Mr. Ross Kendall! Why won't you get out of my head?* She groaned inwardly. How could a man she barely knew wreak such havoc on her utterly perfect and sedate life? This intrusion was certainly most unwelcome.

Just at that very moment, the end of class buzzer sounded. Saved by the bell, she thought wearily.

Slower than usual, the twenty students of the senior English class gathered their books and other belongings and rose from their seats. In their plaid skirts and well-cut navy wool jackets emblazoned with the Perryville crest, they seemed the classic image of immaculately groomed, demure young ladies. Never mind the fact that each successive generation of teenagers always seemed more worldly and sophisticated than the one that had preceded it, Melinda thought with a faint half smile.

"Just one thing, girls," she called out quickly. "Don't forget those short story assignments are due tomorrow."

As expected, there was the usual chorus of groans and sighs from the departing students. Involuntarily Melinda's lips twitched. "Naturally," she added, "to those of you who plan on showing up empty-handed, I again look forward to your usual imaginative if not wildly improbable excuses."

The class shuffled out into the hallway. "So what do you think?" Brenda murmured to Lonnie.

"A guy. She was definitely thinking about a guy," the senior class president whispered confidently.

"It must be that gorgeous hunk, Peter Harrison," declared a third girl. "They make the cutest couple."

"No wonder Miss Clarke was daydreaming," Brenda exclaimed. "He's just totally adorable!"

"Peter Harrison," sighed Lonnie dramatically. "Be still, my beating heart!" Once again, the cluster of teenagers erupted into a fit of delighted giggles that echoed down the long hallway.

I wonder what *that's* all about, Melinda wondered vaguely as she stood in the empty classroom. It had to be about boys, she finally decided. Girls of that age were forever thinking and talking about boys. Hmm, now who was she kidding? Girls of *every* age were always thinking about boys, Melinda admitted reluctantly. Still, she would have been astonished to learn that her students had actually been discussing the rather obvious physical attributes of Peter Harrison. She would have been further astonished to discover that the Perryville Academy student body had almost unanimously decided that it was simply a matter of time before Miss Melinda Clarke, the most popular teacher in the entire school, married the handsomest young bachelor in the county.

Normally Melinda took a great deal of pleasure in her work at the academy. There were so many rewards to be found in teaching such bright and spirited young minds. Her days were often long ones, filled with numerous other activities besides classes. Her duties also included being the adviser on the student literary journal and overseeing several independent study projects for specially gifted students. But the disturbing events of last night had left Melinda tense and emotionally drained, so she was rather grateful that her after-school schedule today was relatively light. She returned to her office shortly after three o'clock, noting with relief that Selene Monroe's chair was unoccupied. The woman was still down in the auditorium with the junior poetry club. Melinda shook her head, trying to imagine her surly office-mate as a kind, patient teacher of elementary school children. It was not a picture that came easily to mind.

She sighed and idly twisted the long, blond French braid that had impressed her older students as the very height of glamor. To Melinda, of course, the sophisticated hairstyle was simply part of an attempt to appear neat and efficient. It went along with the pencil-slim gray skirt and cream silk tailored blouse, which were the envy of her colleagues. She reached for her cashmere coat, the same one she had worn the previous evening. It was exquisitely made, in the classic polo style, and had been the cause of numerous comments by certain jealous members of the staff who considered Melinda Clarke to be a "clotheshorse." But such deprecating remarks did not faze her. In truth, Melinda actually owned very few items of clothing. The outfits she did possess were fashion classics that she wore year after year; they never went out of style. The expensive cashmere coat, in fact, had been a hand-me-down from Liza Langley, who had herself received it as a birthday gift years ago and had scarcely ever worn it.

"Heck, Lindy," Liz had said with a shrug, "give me an old sweatshirt and a pair of faded jeans, any day."

Smiling at the memory, Melinda threw the coat across her shoulders. It was all very well for her childhood friend to dress with tomboy aplomb in the remote rural community of Half Moon Falls, where she now lived in wedded bliss with her handsome husband, Jacob Van Cleef. As the daughter of Arthur Langley, Liza had grown up in the spotlight, as a glamorous debutante and hostess for her famous father. Less than one year ago, she had even been engaged to marry a United States senator. In a startling turn of events, Liza had broken off the engagement, shed her celebrity status as a jet-setter and nestled happily into her new role as the wife of a wealthy farmer.

But Melinda's own situation was far different. As the decidedly unglamorous Little Lindy, she had quite a reputation to live down. Even though sweatshirts and jeans were more her own style than silk blouses and cashmere coats, Melinda was determined to stay as far away from her notorious comic-strip image as possible. Little Lindy had hated dresses and skirts and had adored bright, neon colors, tattered denim and boys' high-top sneakers.

Melinda strode out of the old brick building and over toward the parking area, amidst a bustle of after-school activity. The field hockey, track and archery teams were all conducting afternoon practice. Out of the corner of her eye, Melinda could see Brenda Matthews demonstrating to Lonnie Ellison the correct way to apply press-on nails. Lonnie, in turn, was demonstrating to her best friend the proper method of blowing smoke rings with menthol cigarettes. Melinda shook her head, and opened the door of the car.

She had just pulled out of the long, tree-lined driveway leading to the main road, when she noticed a small, forlorn figure in a Perryville school uniform trudging beside the pavement. With some degree of concern, she drove past the little girl, who appeared to be no older than nine or ten, and studied the child in her rearview mirror. There were several hundred students at the academy, and this particular face did not seem familiar. Then again, Melinda's classes consisted mostly of the older girls. She paused. Even though the young face was not a familiar one, it seemed strikingly unhappy. That was enough to make up her mind. Melinda stepped out of the car.

"Do you know who I am?" she asked gently.

The girl stared up at her in surprise. "You're Miss Clarke."

"Good, because you shouldn't talk to strangers."

"You're not a stranger. Everybody knows who you are." The child sounded almost awestruck.

Melinda suppressed a smile. "I hope you don't mind my asking, but what are you doing on this road by yourself?"

The little girl evaded her eyes. "I'm walking."

"Walking where?"

"Home."

Melinda raised an eyebrow. "Home?" There were very few day pupils at the Perryville Academy. Most of the students lived at one of the several ivy-covered dormitories on the campus grounds. Reading the obvious misery on this youngster's face, Melinda thought it was possible she was dealing with another student who simply wanted to run away from school.

Tactfully she inquired, "Why didn't you take the school bus?"

"Um, I missed it."

"You missed it?" Melinda smiled. "Well then, it's fortunate I happened to come along. I can give you a ride home."

"Okay!" The girl beamed happily. "I live just down that road over there...."

Melinda shook her head in puzzlement. So she really had just been walking home! "What is your name, dear?"

"Jenny."

She took note of the girl's cultured English accent. "Tell me, Jenny. Are you new at the academy?"

"Yes."

"And do you like our school?"

"No." The reply was brief yet revealing.

"Why not?"

Jenny lowered her brown eyes to the pavement. "You said you would give me a ride home, Miss Clarke."

"So I did." Melinda gestured to the passenger side. "Hop in. Now, what's the name of the street you live on?"

As the child gave directions, Melinda wondered what was the cause of her apparent unhappiness. Surely it couldn't be just school. She was such a solemn-looking little girl, with strange hollows in her cheeks and the faintest of shadows beneath her eyes. Melinda recalled herself at approximately that same age. Bright blue eyes aglow with mischief and a perpetual smile on her chubby face. The quintessential image of Little Lindy.

After several moments of silence, Melinda turned to her passenger and murmured, "I couldn't help but wonder, Jenny. Today is Thursday. Don't you have any special after-school activities?"

Jenny's lips tightened. "I don't have to go if I don't want to."

Now we're getting somewhere, she thought. "Go where?"

"Miss Monroe's junior poetry club. I'm not going!"

Melinda was careful not to reveal her own opinion on the subject of Miss Selene Monroe. "Well, look," she murmured at last, "I'm sure there are other activities you might prefer instead of poetry."

"I like poetry. I hate Miss Monroe!"

"Whatever," was Melinda's bland reply. Melinda was determined to have a little talk with Jenny's parents when she brought the child home.

Melinda had been so lost in thought that she didn't realize at first how strangely familiar the curving country road actually was. Then the startling thought occurred to her.

"This is where you live?"

"Yes."

Melinda stared in astonishment at the rambling landmark colonial on the top of the hill. It was the same mansion she had been to just the night before. It belonged to Ross Kendall. She studied her young companion's face. "What is your last name, Jenny?"

"Kendall."

I should have known, she groaned inwardly. Bizarre coincidence such as this one always seemed to happen in the "Life With Lindy" comic strip. Since when was real life any different? Besides, Melinda chided herself, how could she have possibly failed to notice the family resemblance? Jenny Kendall had her father's same haunting brown eyes. So, this was the daughter Peter had mentioned briefly. The one who had been living all these years with her mother in Europe.

Melinda brought her vintage blue Mustang convertible to a stop in the center of the circular driveway.

"Thank you very much for the ride, Miss Clarke,"
Jenny Kendall said in her soft, polite voice.

Melinda nodded, still unsure what to do next. Just
a moment ago, she had been firm in her resolve to
speak with this unhappy child's parents and make
them aware of what might have been a potentially
dangerous situation. What if she hadn't happened to
drive by when she had? Even in a tranquil town such
as Perryville, there was still a certain degree of risk for
a little girl walking alone on a heavily traveled public
road. Melinda was torn between her concern for
Jenny Kendall and her reluctance to face the child's
father. Seeing that insufferable man again could
prove to be extremely awkward.

With sudden relief, she realized there was no other
car in the driveway. She glanced at her watch. Of
course—it was only three-thirty! Obviously Mr. Ross
Kendall was still at his office. Good, Melinda decided. She would avoid a potentially uncomfortable
confrontation. The simple solution was to call him on
the telephone later in the evening. That way, she could
still discuss Jenny without having to face the man.

A plump, middle-aged woman in a gray-and-white
uniform suddenly appeared in the doorway and stared
at Melinda's car with undisguised curiosity.

"That's Miriam," explained Jenny, giving a wave
as she opened the passenger door.

Somewhat reluctantly Melinda emerged from the
vehicle. Responding to the housekeeper's question-
ing stare, she walked up the steps and shook her hand.
"Hello. My name is Melinda Clarke and I'm a teacher
at Jenny's school."

To her surprise, the other woman smiled broadly. "I remember you, Miss Clarke."

"You do?"

"From the party last night. You came with that attractive young Mr. Harrison."

"Oh, right." Melinda hesitated uneasily. "I was wondering—could I leave a message for Mr. Kendall?"

"Sure." Miriam nodded. "But if you have anything to say to the boss, why not tell him yourself?" She pointed her finger. "He's just coming up the driveway now."

With a sudden lurch in her stomach, Melinda turned to see a green Jaguar pull up behind her own car. Great. Terrific. *This* was all she needed!

Ross Kendall emerged from his car, looking every inch the successful banker in a custom-tailored three-piece suit. Dark aviator glasses concealed his eyes.

"Hi, Daddy!"

"Hello, sweetheart." He bent down to kiss his daughter, but was unable to stop staring at the young woman who stood behind her. "Melinda," he murmured under his breath. She was undoubtedly the last person in the world he had expected to find standing in his driveway.

"Mr. Kendall." Melinda nodded perfunctorily, making every effort to appear calm and unruffled. Heavens, she thought unhappily, the man was even more devastating in the afternoon sunlight!

"Miss Clarke gave me a ride home," Jenny explained.

"Is that so?" He looked at her questioningly.

There was an uncomfortable silence. "Apparently Jenny missed the school bus." She felt his unseen eyes burning into her.

Perhaps sensing the tension in the air, Miriam gave a bright smile and took Jenny by the hand. "I baked your favorite cookies this afternoon."

"Oatmeal chocolate chip?" the little girl inquired hopefully.

"But of course!" The older woman nodded matter-of-factly. "Why don't we go inside and have some with milk?"

"Can we invite Miss Clarke, too?"

"Most definitely," interjected Ross Kendall with a twist of his lips.

"I . . . I really must be going—" Melinda said hastily.

"Trying to make a clean getaway?" he challenged softly.

"Uh, not at all!" She tried to avoid his gaze. "It's getting late and I have a few errands to run."

"I don't doubt it." Ross's mouth tightened. He turned to his daughter. "Sweetheart, why don't you go and have those cookies now. Maybe I can convince Miss Clarke to join us a little later."

"Okay!"

A few moments later, Jenny had gone into the house with Miriam. That left Melinda standing alone with Ross Kendall in the center of the driveway. There was an awkward pause. Finally he spoke up. "I didn't think I was going to see you again."

Melinda hesitated. "Please understand, this has nothing whatsoever to do with last night."

"No?"

"No."

"I see." His tone was deceptively bland.

"It just so happened that Jenny needed a ride home."

"Oh." Pensively he removed his sunglasses.

"I had no idea she was your daughter."

His eyes glimmered. "And would that have made a difference?"

"No." She felt the burn of that brown gaze. "Of course not."

"Well, then. I suppose I just ought to say thank you, and leave it at that."

Melinda paused uncomfortably. "Wait."

"Oh, was there something else you wanted to say to me, Melinda?" Ross Kendall's mouth twisted ironically.

"As a matter of fact, yes."

"I can't imagine what on earth you would possibly have to tell me, unless you plan on adding to your litany of kind words from last night. Let's see, there was egotistical, arrogant, bad judge of character... what else?"

Her cheeks flushed. "I already told you, Mr. Kendall. This is not about last night."

He leaned his lanky frame against the shiny green sedan. "Then what exactly are we talking about?"

"We're talking about Jenny."

"Jenny?"

Melinda crossed her arms. "When I found your daughter, she was walking, all by herself, nearly half a mile away from the school grounds."

"She was *what?*" There was astonishment in Ross Kendall's voice.

"She claimed to have missed the bus."

His expression hardened. "What the hell kind of school can't keep track of young children? Do you have any idea what might have happened if—"

"There's no need to bite *my* head off, Mr. Kendall," Melinda snapped. "I'm the one who brought Jenny home, remember?"

"I haven't forgotten," came the quiet reply. "I owe you for that one, Melinda."

"You don't owe me anything."

"Don't I?"

She thrust her hands into the pockets of her polo coat. "What would you possibly owe me?"

He took a step toward her. "To start with, an apology."

"An apology for what?"

"I got the distinct impression that you were...insulted last evening. That was never my intention, believe me."

"Forget it."

"What if I don't want to forget it?" There was a strange vulnerability to his words that startled Melinda.

Suddenly her throat felt dry. "I came here to discuss your daughter."

"All right, what about her?" The question seemed torn from his lips.

"Mr. Kendall, I don't normally make a habit of involving myself in other people's affairs."

"That much is obvious."

Melinda glanced at him sharply. "The point is, Jenny is obviously having a difficult time adjusting to her new school."

"I know."

"If she were a student of mine, I might be in a better position to help. Unfortunately, as things stand now—"

He nodded. "You teach only the older girls."

"That's right." She looked surprised.

"What kind of a person is this Selene Monroe?"

Oh, wonderful! She groaned inwardly. All she needed was to stir up a hornet's nest involving her moody office-mate. Wasn't life with the woman miserable enough?

"Your silence is deafening."

"Uh, well, actually, I'm not the right person to ask."

"I have a feeling that you're *precisely* the person to ask."

Drat the man and his uncanny powers of perception! "Look, you're putting me in an awkward position."

"I seem to make a habit of that, don't I?" he murmured cryptically. "Look, I understand that she's your colleague, but strictly off the record—what's your honest opinion of this Monroe woman? Jenny seems to dislike her intensely."

"Then I strongly suggest you arrange a parent-teacher conference with Miss Monroe and draw your own conclusions."

"I fully intend to."

In the stark afternoon sunlight, the scars of his gaunt face seemed even more vivid. Melinda found herself wondering about the terrible secret that lay hidden behind them. Unexpectedly she felt the stirrings of compassion for Ross Kendall and what he must have suffered. This sudden welling up of emotion made her distinctly uncomfortable. She cleared her throat. "Uh, I really must be going."

"Wait."

Nervously Melinda made the pretense of glancing down at her wristwatch. "It's getting late, and—"

He effectively blocked her path. "I want to ask you something." After the briefest hesitation, Ross continued. "What would Little Lindy do?"

"Little Lindy?"

"You heard me."

"Why on earth are you bringing *that* up?"

"Why, indeed. Because I sincerely believe my daughter could learn a great deal from your...alter ego."

She winced. "Don't call that obnoxious cartoon character my alter ego."

"I'm just being honest."

"Oh? Well, who the heck asked you to be honest? I certainly don't recall soliciting such an opinion from you, Mr. Kendall!"

"Do you have any idea how your eyes flash when you get angry?"

"Kindly do not change the subject!"

He reached out and touched her French braid playfully. "You know, I like your hair even better when it's down this way."

The light touch of his hand caused the oddest sensation in the pit of Melinda's stomach. "And what in heaven's name could you possibly think Jenny could learn from a demon like Lindy?"

Ross smiled faintly. "Aren't you being a little hard on yourself? I always found Little Lindy a rather spirited and delightful creature."

"How many times do I have to tell you? *I'm* not Lindy!"

"But you *were,* once."

"That was very long ago."

His smile broadened. "I doubt it. You're still quite young. Why make it sound like ancient history?"

"Because as far as I'm concerned, it *is* ancient history!"

"I don't understand. Why deny something that's such a part of yourself?"

"I already told you, Mr. Kendall. It's taken me a long time to live down my Little Lindy days."

"And I already told *you*—the name is Ross."

"Whatever."

"Not whatever. *Ross,*" he insisted. "What is it going to take to get you to call me by my first name? Have you any idea how old it makes me feel when you call me Mr. Kendall?"

Again, Melinda found her mind wandering. How old was Ross Kendall? she wondered. The lines that crinkled at the corners of his eyes and mouth seemed more a result of exposure to the sun than age. The man couldn't be more than thirty-four at the most, she estimated.

"I'm thirty-five," he answered quietly.

"Have you always been a mind reader?"

"Not until very recently." Melinda looked unexpectedly lovely in the daylight. The soft colors of her coat and blouse flattered her peaches-and-cream complexion. She wore less makeup than on the previous evening, and combined with that different hairstyle, it made her appear younger and far less sophisticated. Whatever miracle of fate had brought Melinda back to his home after last night's debacle, Ross was determined to take full advantage of the situation. He had to find some way to make her stay longer. With a sinking feeling, Ross realized that she obviously couldn't wait to leave. He could hear the sound of Melinda's car keys as she jiggled them nervously in between her slender fingers. How intently she kept staring down at the fine white gravel of the driveway, unwilling to look him directly in the eyes. That made matters even worse, Ross thought bitterly, to know that he made a woman so uncomfortable. That he was so unappealing, so unattractive, so utterly hard to look at. At that moment, he would have given his entire fortune to have a different face, a handsome face. A face like Peter Harrison. "Melinda," he began, his voice strained, "would it be asking too much for you to stay just a little longer?"

An odd sensation washed over her. "To discuss . . . Jenny?"

"Yes." Ross tried to sound matter-of-fact. "What else would we have to discuss?"

She hesitated. "I'm not sure if it's wise for me to interfere—"

"Listen, I realize you don't approve of me, but—"

"I never said I didn't approve of you."

"Not in so many words," came the taut reply, "but you've made it quite clear that you don't care for me personally."

"Don't put words in my mouth."

He shrugged. "There's no need to be tactful, Melinda. I'm well aware that you have a low opinion of me. However, we happen to be talking about my child. As far as I'm concerned, that's a completely different issue."

The man truly believed she disliked him, Melinda thought in amazement. How could she possibly explain to Ross Kendall that her harsh words last evening had been spoken in anger and failed to reveal a deeper truth. That she found him tantalizingly attractive. And now, standing in such close proximity to his undeniable maleness, Melinda was quite unprepared for the havoc it wreaked on her senses. After more than twenty-four years of considering herself cool and unflappable, she was distinctly uncomfortable with this new and disturbing sensation. And just when she had nearly convinced herself that the man's magnetic effect on her last night had been merely a product of an overactive imagination. More unwelcome thoughts continued to invade Melinda's mind. Such as, what would it be like to feel Ross Kendall's hard mouth on hers? What would it be like to be held against the strength of his tall, muscular body while they danced alone in the April moonlight—*Good grief, what in the world had gotten into her all of a sudden? Since when had the mere presence of a man reduced her to jelly? It never would have happened to Little Lindy!*

Melinda wondered if Ross Kendall was aware of the tumult that he was causing. Had he even the slightest clue?

"Please, Melinda," he urged beguilingly, "stay for milk and cookies."

"Well..." Her resolve started to weaken.

"It would make Jenny very happy." Ross fired the final salvo. "And that's a rare occurrence these days."

"Milk and cookies, hmm?" Melinda smiled in spite of herself.

"Oatmeal chocolate chip." His eyes twinkled. "How can you possibly pass up a deal like that, Miss Clarke?"

Despite all her previous misgivings, it developed into the most pleasant afternoon Melinda had spent in a long while. Last night, the historic, sprawling Kendall mansion had been crowded, noisy and impersonal. Today, with just Ross Kendall, his daughter and the two members of his household staff, it was a different place altogether. Melinda could take the time to appreciate that this truly was a *home*. After setting up the milk, coffee and cookies in the charming breakfast nook, Miriam and Willis exchanged conspiratorial winks and melted away tactfully.

Strangely enough, Ross didn't have much to say. He just sat quietly and watched Jenny blossom like a flower in the gentle company of Melinda Clarke. No wonder she was so well-liked, he marveled. It was hardly a surprise that such a person was considered the most popular teacher in the entire school. Melinda possessed the rare ability to draw even the most introverted child out. She not only listened, but seemed to understand youngsters, without appearing to patronize them.

"And then, there's the summer cottage on Long Island Sound...." The normally untalkative Jenny was chattering away. "Daddy says it has its own private beach. As soon as school's over, we're going to spend the whole summer there."

Melinda smiled as she munched another chewy cookie. "That sounds terrific."

"I wish we didn't have to wait that long, Miss Clarke," the little girl confided. "I wish we could go tomorrow."

"A month isn't really such a long time."

"It seems like forever." Jenny sighed.

"When I was your age, a month did seem like forever," Melinda conceded. "But believe me when I tell you the weeks will pass in no time."

"Do you really think so?"

"Absolutely." Melinda nodded affirmatively.

Jenny turned to the third person at the dining table and declared, "Daddy, you told me there's lots of room at the beach house. Couldn't Miss Clarke come, too?"

Melinda turned a bright shade of pink at exactly the moment Ross started choking on his coffee.

"Did I say something wrong?" Jenny looked back and forth at the two adults in bewilderment.

"Of course not," Melinda murmured hastily.

"Absolutely not," Ross assured his daughter. With the greatest effort, he managed to set down his china coffee mug without spilling the contents. "Miss Clarke is welcome to visit us at the shore cottage any time she wants."

"That's so great!" Jenny was ecstatic. "What do you say, Miss Clarke?"

Ross cleared his throat briskly. "Don't you have homework to do?"

"Yes, Daddy."

"Well?"

The little girl beamed. "I'm glad you could stay for tea, Miss Clarke." With a bright wave, she disappeared upstairs to her room.

Ross was silent for a long moment. "That's the first time I've seen her smile in ages."

"She's a very sweet child."

"But not a happy one. I suppose you've noticed the shadows under her eyes." There was a pained expression on his face. "My daughter doesn't sleep very well these days."

"I'm sorry." Melinda's compassion was genuine. There was still so much she didn't know about the girl, but an inner sense told her this was not the time to pry.

"She likes you very much."

"And I like her."

He stared at her strangely. "Melinda, what if—"

"If what?"

"Do you think we might still—" The words died away. Abruptly Ross stood up from the table. "It's late. I'm sure you're anxious to get home."

Oddly Melinda wasn't anxious to be anywhere else at the present time. In the past hour, she had seen a side of the blunt-speaking banker that seemed totally unexpected. A devoted, gentle parent. And she had found that oddly touching. "Oh, is it late?"

His smile was grim. "It's not necessary to be polite. I'm sure you can't wait to leave."

She folded her arms in a defiant pose. "You're quite sure of a lot of things, aren't you, Mr. Ross Kendall?"

He blinked. "I'll walk you to your car."

What was it he had been about to ask before? Melinda wondered as the two of them walked through the center hall. Why did the man suddenly seem so tense? Surreptitiously, she stole a glance at Ross as he accompanied her in silence down the stone steps leading into the driveway. The undamaged side of his gaunt face was in profile. There remained a harsh, strained quality to those features.

Then, it happened. She was so intent on studying her companion, that Melinda lost her footing and stumbled, missing the next step completely. She would have fallen headlong down the remaining stairs, if a pair of powerful arms had not reached out and caught her in midair.

"Oh!" She gasped in surprise against the athletic hardness of Ross Kendall's tall frame.

"I've got you," he murmured, but did not release her.

Was he actually trembling? Melinda marveled. "You...you can let me go, now," she whispered shakily. The fine wool material of his expensive gray suit would not conceal a tension coiled tight as a spring.

"Do you have any idea how good you feel against me?" Ross pressed his lips into the silk of her hair.

"Please, Mr. Kendall!" At first she wanted to struggle against the uninvited embrace, but a delicious lethargy had already begun to invade her traitorous body.

"*Mr.* Kendall?" he uttered hoarsely. "What in heaven's name is it going to take to get you to say my name properly?"

It had never felt quite like this when Peter or any other man had held her. What on earth was causing this exquisite little shudder along the nape of her neck? Could it be Ross Kendall's warm breath fanning the delicate bare skin?

"Don't do that!" came the faint protest.

His eyes glimmered. "Do what?"

Almost in slow motion, his taut mouth lowered toward her own. Any moment now, he would kiss her. And in that brief instant, Melinda realized it was what she wanted. "Ross!" Her gaze locked with his.

"At last." A flutter of a laugh escaped from his throat. "Say it again—say my name!"

"Ross—" All at once, she relaxed against his masculine strength, surrendering slowly to this devastating assault on her senses.

Ross gave a low exclamation of surprise as he felt the stirrings of her response. "Melinda!"

"What?" It was little more than a whisper.

He stared at her flushed cheeks and drew in his breath. "I think we'd better quit while we're ahead, don't you?" With an odd tremor, he released her from the dizzying embrace. Abruptly Ross turned on his heels, and without another word, disappeared back inside the rambling, colonial mansion.

Chapter Five

It was all in her mind, Melinda assured herself flatly for the one hundredth time. She was just overreacting to the potent charms of an extremely experienced Lothario. What on earth was wrong with her? Had she actually taken leave of her senses, almost allowing Ross Kendall to kiss her like that?

Melinda pushed away the casserole she had heated up for dinner in the small microwave. She simply wasn't hungry tonight. Idly she clicked on the remote control and briefly scanned the channels of the television. In another moment, she shut off the power. There was nothing to interest her, no way of distracting her mind from the tumult that seemed to have overtaken her life in the past twenty-four hours. The cause of all this inner turmoil could be described in two simple words: Ross Kendall. Melinda wrapped her terry-cloth robe more tightly around her chilled body. She didn't like feeling this way, not one bit. It was too new, too disturbing. There had never been a single night in her life when she had had trouble sleeping. When the thought of a certain man, or any man for that matter, had invaded her heart and mind.

She sighed and glanced regretfully around the quaint, cozy apartment. Up until yesterday, her world had seemed so perfectly ordered, so comfortably controlled. Melinda shook her head in frustration. At times like this, she sorely missed having a friend to talk with, to confide in. But only a handful of people knew the truth. How after nearly eighteen years of behaving like an unruly tomboy, Melinda had suddenly taken a look around her and decided she no longer wanted to be the notorious Little Lindy. She wanted to be just like everyone else. During that first semester away at college, she learned what it meant to be "one of the girls." With the help of Liza Langley, Melinda was even accepted into a sorority. During that time, she acquired a polish and feminine confidence that astounded her family. It was a role Melinda had come to savor far more than the irresponsible Little Lindy. How totally refreshing to be viewed as a model of decorum. As a demure and proper young lady. How utterly tranquil it made her life!

"I liked her better the old way," grumbled her brother Gareth into his pipe at Thanksgiving dinner two years ago.

"Remember the time she blew up Dad's lab and we ended up taking the blame?" sighed Wyler wistfully as he passed the platter of sweet potatoes.

"What about the moat she tried to dig around the house?" grinned Devlin. "Those were the days!"

Those were the days, indeed! Melinda forced her mind back to the present with a grimace on her face. No one had been happier than she to see the "good old days" disappear forever. It wasn't as if she had been the only person in the Clarke family to change so radically. Her three older brothers had also managed to metamorphose into rather serious adults. Devlin had become a scientist, Wyler was a successful author, and Gareth? Well, it seemed Gareth did something for the government that was so highly classified that even Arthur Langley didn't know much about it. *Supposedly.*

Anyhow, the point was, the Clarke children had all grown up. Most important, the infamous Little Lindy had grown up. It was therefore exceedingly disturbing to discover that there was a man out there who was capable of upsetting Melinda's very proper new life. Until that fateful meeting with Ross Kendall, no one had ever gotten under her skin. Until last night's blatant attempt at seduction, she had sincerely believed herself to be better off with a man like Peter Harrison. No surprises, and no somersaults in her stomach whenever he touched her. *Unlike Ross Kendall.* How could she possibly forget the incident on the steps this afternoon? Why even bother to deny that being held so intimately by the man had been such an unexpectedly shattering experience?

Nervously Melinda trudged over to the tiny refrigerator and flung open the freezer door. A minute later, she was leaning against the counter with a half-eaten container of gourmet chocolate marshmallow ice cream in her hand. And why even bother to deny, she thought as she munched unhappily, that she had wanted Ross to kiss her? It had been almost like an ache. When he had broken off the embrace so abruptly Melinda had been both disappointed and relieved. She had begun to feel like a moth at a flame. And that was far too dangerous for her well-being. Never in her life had Melinda ever felt such a strange vulnerability. The warning buzzer had sounded loudly as those hard lips had descended toward hers. A million alarm bells had gone off in her head. But it had been a false alarm, after all. Ross Kendall had been the one to pull away at the last minute. All that much better, she thought assertively, tossing the empty ice-cream carton into the trash. The last thing she needed in her life right now was a mesmerizing, cocksure playboy like Ross Kendall.

Certainly, absolutely not! With Peter, her life would continue to be easygoing and comfortable. And there was no reason in the world why Peter ever had to find out about today's harmless little incident on the steps leading to Ross Kendall's driveway. Ross might have held her so tightly that it had quite taken Melinda's breath away. The man probably did that sort of thing all the time. But it was not going to happen again with her. Hadn't he even agreed? He had declared, "We'd better quit while we're ahead." A very wise sentiment.

By the time Saturday night rolled around, Melinda was convinced that any special chemistry that might have existed between herself and Ross Kendall was merely a figment of her imagination. Like any other mild flirtation, it had run its brief course, and now evaporated back into thin air.

She had decided to wear an elegant but casual outfit for her movie date with Peter. An oversized powder-blue angora sweater, black silk slacks and a pair of simple black patent flats. In keeping with the relaxed mood of the evening, Melinda brushed her blond hair to fall in long, loose waves. She had just finished applying a sheer pink-tinted lip gloss when the telephone rang.

She hastily reached for the receiver, quite sure it was Peter informing her that he was running a little late. "Hi!" she said with a hint of laughter.

"Hello, Melinda." The deep voice on the other line did not belong to Peter Harrison."

"Ross." She tried not to betray her astonishment.

"Listen." He seemed to hesitate. "I realize it's at the last minute, but would you like to go out this evening with Jenny and me?"

"This evening?" Melinda repeated in an odd tone.

"We could all grab a bite to eat or something."

At that precise moment the doorbell rang. "It's very kind of you to ask," she stammered into the receiver, "but—"

"You don't have to finish that sentence," Ross interrupted in a dry, cynical tone. "I can hear the doorbell."

What else could she say? For some inexplicable reason, Melinda felt oddly regretful. The prospect of a family-type evening out with Ross and his gentle little daughter seemed rather appealing. "I'm sorry that I already have plans."

Despite all her previous assertions about Ross Kendall, had Melinda not already been committed to tonight's date with Peter, she would have found it difficult to turn down the older man's surprising invitation.

"Forget it. I'm sorry to have bothered you." Ross closed the conversation with stiff politeness, "Perhaps another time."

"Yes. Another time, perhaps," Melinda echoed quietly. The doorbell rang again insistently. "All right, just a minute!" she called out with mild impatience. *Another time.* She replaced the receiver with a strange feeling in the pit of her stomach. Now, what were the odds of Ross Kendall ever asking her out again? Melinda made her way to the front door. She corrected herself. The man hadn't exactly asked her out. At least, not on a date, anyway. Why make such a big deal of it? He obviously sensed how much Jenny seemed to enjoy her company. The child was new in town and had no friends of her own age yet. Why read anything personal into the invitation? Ross Kendall knew his daughter was shy and lonely. He was merely behaving like any concerned, devoted father.

Melinda forced the thought of Ross Kendall from her mind and opened the front door with a bright smile. "Sorry to take so long."

Peter stood there, looking rather attractive in a cream-colored fisherman's sweater and dark corduroy slacks. "Well worth the wait," he declared with a boyish smile and took her in his arms. "You look especially pretty tonight." He kissed her lightly on the lips.

For a moment, Melinda let herself yield to the kiss. The young lawyer exuded the heady, cloying scent of an imported lime cologne. Before she could think how little electricity there was in the touch of his mouth, Peter pulled back from the brief embrace with a self-satisfied expression on his handsome face. "Now, what more could any man ask?"

The Perryville Cinema was like so many old movie houses found in small towns throughout America. Unlike many bustling suburban areas, where the exquisitely ornate art deco theaters of the twenties and thirties had long since been replaced with the stark, boxlike structures favored by the large film chains, the Perryville Cinema remained unchanged over the years. The walls were still draped in the same faded crimson velvet, elaborate plaster scrollwork arched toward the high ceiling to frame a deep blue sky painted with perfect, dreamlike clouds. There was scarcely a soul in Perryville between the ages of fifteen and seventy-five who hadn't exchanged their first kiss in the shadowy, secluded balcony. Young people had considered the Perryville Cinema the hub of all romantic dating activity for generations.

Tonight was no different. Melinda looked around the crowded theater and recognized many of her students from the academy. They all acknowledged her with a wave and an occasional giggle.

"It's really packed," Peter murmured in between munches of buttered popcorn. "Everybody wants to see the new Wendell Wynberg extravaganza."

"Oh, sure...that must be it," she said with a wry smile.

"Naturally I've read the book that this movie is based on. Have you read *Enchanted Galaxies?* I can't wait to see it." He balanced the oversized tub of popcorn awkwardly in his lap and reached across the seat to place a casual arm around Melinda.

It was pleasant, very pleasant, she thought vaguely. Peter Harrison was a pleasant person, she repeated to herself for the tenth time. So what if he had a piece of popcorn stuck between his two front teeth? Why was it so suddenly annoying to notice the way he whistled along with all the piped-in theater music?

Two hours later, the house lights came up and the theater was alive with the deafening buzz of a cheerful audience.

"Wasn't that terrific?" Peter stood up to leave. "Jake Wills has always been my favorite actor."

"Mine, too." There was nothing like the happy feeling one received from a satisfying and exciting film, Melinda thought. It had been said that Wendell Wynberg, probably the most successful producer-director in the world, refused to make a picture with a sad ending.

"Thanks for taking me, Peter. That's one movie I could certainly sit through twice."

He beamed. "I'm glad you enjoyed it. So, where would you like to grab a bite?"

The two of them were still considering different places for a late-evening snack as they followed the crowd out into the lobby. Just when Peter was placing a proprietary arm around Melinda to guide her through the exit doors, she heard a familiar high voice.

"Look, Daddy—there's Miss Clarke!"

Startled, she turned to see a delighted Jenny Kendall standing with a craggy-faced man whose curt nod of greeting was as chilly as the Arctic Ocean. Ross Kendall looked uncharacteristically casual in a corduroy sports jacket and faded dungarees.

"Good evening, Mr. Kendall." Peter acknowledged his firm's most influential client with just the proper note of awe and respect.

"Mr. Harrison." There was the slightest hesitation, before he added, "Miss Clarke."

"Hello, Jenny." Melinda's expression warmed as she turned from the coldness of Ross Kendall's stare.

"Isn't this funny, Miss Clarke?" the little girl chattered happily. "Imagine all of us being here at the same time... I loved this movie, didn't you? I can't wait till it comes out on video..."

Peter tightened his arm possessively around Melinda's waist, completely oblivious to the fact that the older man's jaw tightened. "I didn't know you knew Mr. Kendall's daughter," he remarked vaguely.

"She's a teacher at my school." Jenny looked at him as if he had just arrived from the planet Mars. "*Everybody* knows Miss Clarke!"

"Oh, well, of course," Peter agreed offhandedly. He was already more concerned with finding a way to parlay this chance social encounter with Ross Kendall into a profitable opportunity to "network." He cleared his throat. "Mr. Kendall, would the two of you care to join us for some dinner?"

"Please, Daddy." Jenny tugged eagerly at her father's sleeve. "Say we can!"

Ross stared grimly at Melinda. "I don't know, pumpkin. After all, we wouldn't want to intrude on this young couple's date."

"Oh, no! You wouldn't be intruding at all!" Peter asserted hastily. "Would they, Melinda?"

"Oh, of course not." There was the slightest trace of sarcasm in her voice.

"Please?" Jenny implored her father once again.

The briefest look of tenderness crossed Ross's face as he regarded his daughter's hopeful, pleading eyes. "Very well," came the taut response. "Jenny and I would be delighted to join you."

The four of them were wedged into a small booth at the bright and noisy Perryville Pizza Parlor, Ross and Jenny on one side, with Melinda and Peter on the other. In the center of the tiny table were the remains of a huge sausage-and-mushroom pizza. Amidst the deafening rock music that blared out of the classic fifties jukebox, Jenny Kendall was continuing to talk a blue streak.

"...And then there was this other girl whose father commuted from London to Paris every day, can you imagine that?"

"Amazing," murmured Melinda with an affectionate smile. It warmed her heart to see the shy young girl chattering on this way. If only Ross Kendall weren't here to make her feel so positively unnerved. He had sat through the entire meal in stony silence, making only the most minimal contribution to the general conversation.

"...But I guess in the United States, a commute from New York to Philadelphia is really the same thing, right?"

"Absolutely," Melinda agreed, "and do you want to know something else, Jenny? When you get better acquainted, the other girls in your class will be very impressed with all the fascinating things you can tell them about living in another country."

"Do you really think so?"

"I *know* so."

It was rather decent of Melinda to encourage Jenny like this, Ross was forced to confess. So far, his own efforts with the child had seemed woefully inadequate. Yet, in one brief afternoon, this young woman had singlehandedly and effortlessly managed to bring his troubled daughter out of her shell. But Melinda's tenderness extended only to Jenny and not himself, Ross thought bitterly. Not only did she continue to avoid his eyes, but they had gone back to being "Mr. Kendall" and "Miss Clarke." Could it only have been two days ago that he had held Melinda in his arms? Ross's powerful body almost shuddered. When she had fallen against him so unexpectedly, she had been so soft, and had he imagined it—almost yielding? If Melinda hadn't lost her footing on those slippery marble steps, he might never have dared to take advantage of the situation. Now, sitting across the table and having to watch that idiot Harrison drape his arm around her as if she were his own personal property, was driving Ross crazy.

"By the way, have you taken a look yet at my proposal for the old Humboldt property, Mr. Kendall?"

Peter Harrison's deceptively casual voice annoyed Ross even more.

"No, not yet," he answered curtly. Damn that pretty-boy pip-squeak, Ross grumbled to himself. This jealousy was a new and alien emotion, and he didn't enjoy the experience one bit. Watching Harrison sitting in the booth so cocky and confident, with his arm around Melinda! If he weren't such a gentleman, he might be sorely tempted to punch the young attorney right in that perfectly chiseled nose of his. Ross cursed himself for not hauling off and kissing Melinda when he'd had the chance. But the truth was, he'd been afraid that she would be repulsed by his advances. Hadn't she already made it clear that she wasn't the slightest bit interested in someone like himself? It had taken every bit of willpower Ross possessed to release her from the potent embrace and walk away with some degree of dignity. He still had his pride, didn't he?

Well, not exactly, Ross admitted bleakly. What possibly could he have been thinking just a few hours ago when he had so recklessly phoned Melinda and asked her out on the flimsy pretext of dinner with Jenny and himself? After she had politely and *predictably* turned him down, he'd hung up the receiver in cold embarrassment and cursed his own stupidity. Had he actually taken leave of his senses to assume that someone as sweet and desirable as Melinda Clarke would be sitting home dateless on a Saturday night? Had the past seven years turned him into such an utter moron? Although, come to think of it, he *was* having dinner with Melinda tonight, after all. Ross stifled an urge to glare across the table at Golden

Boy. This cozy little foursome wasn't quite what he'd had in mind, but it would have to do for now.

"I suppose this isn't the best time to discuss the Humboldt proposal." Peter couldn't keep the edge of disappointment out of his voice. This unexpected opportunity to develop a more intimate business relationship with Ross Kendall wasn't working out the way he'd planned. With Melinda encouraging that little chatterbox daughter, Peter had scarcely been able to get a word in edgewise. He made a mental note to gently remind Melinda later about not allowing young children to monopolize what should have been an *adult* conversation. It was all very well for his date to pay attention to the child, but honestly, didn't schoolteachers ever go off duty? Ross Kendall must be finding the entire evening a complete bore. It certainly wasn't his imagination, Peter sighed, that the older man seemed unusually glum tonight. Of course, the wealthy banker was bored to death! What else could it possibly be?

"No, it isn't the best time," Ross agreed solemnly, and continued to gaze at Melinda out of the corner of his eye. *This* was the way she should wear her hair all the time, he thought. All loose and tumbling over her shoulders. He hadn't any idea that those lovely blond waves were so long. He wanted to reach across the narrow table and run his fingers through the silky strands. Isn't that just what Harrison would be doing later tonight when he took Melinda home? The idea of another man touching her so intimately was a torture for Ross. Abruptly he lowered his eyes and stared down at the table top.

Meanwhile, Peter leaned closer to Melinda and murmured, "I could go for another pizza. What about you?"

Her throat was strangely dry. "No, thanks." She hadn't enjoyed her dinner at all. Somehow, with Ross Kendall sitting opposite her in the booth, Melinda's appetite had completely deserted her. The pizza had tasted like sawdust. The man was so uncommunicative, so oddly subdued. Somehow, she had expected more clever repartee and acid wit. Ross delivered neither. He seemed distracted and coldly aloof. But there was still no denying the fact that even sitting there as stone-faced as a statue, he managed to radiate an inner core of vitality—a disturbingly male presence.

"Say, would anyone want something else to eat, or maybe some dessert?" Peter asked genially.

"No, thanks." Ross was stiffly polite.

"Well, how about another pitcher of cola?" the young attorney persisted.

"I don't think so," came the taciturn reply. "In fact, it's getting late."

A contrary imp suddenly possessed Melinda. Wasn't it bad enough that Ross Kendall had practically ruined her date tonight? But worse, the look of disappointment on Jenny's face was enough to break her heart. "Really—" her tone was slightly annoyed "—is it so late?"

Ross raised a surprised eyebrow. "Yes, as far as I'm concerned."

"Nine o'clock on a Saturday night is past your bedtime, Mr. Kendall?"

Peter's jaw practically dropped, but Ross had the faint beginnings of a smile on his lips. "I had no idea you were even remotely interested in when I went to bed, Miss Clarke," he murmured silkily.

Melinda practically choked on her soda. It was all her own fault, she chastised herself, for making such a reckless taunt. Still, she never expected Ross to respond with such an obvious sexual innuendo. Miraculously Peter appeared to be oblivious to the double entendre, and Jenny hadn't even been paying attention. Ross Kendall, however, was another story altogether. It seemed as if a new light had come into his eyes. Deliberately he turned to Peter.

"You know what, Harrison? Come to think of it, I probably *could* eat another pizza!"

"Oh, great!" Peter was immediately revitalized.

And Melinda's deep pink flush did not go unnoticed by Ross. He continued to stare searchingly across the table. "By the way, another pitcher also sounds like a wonderful idea."

It felt almost as if the man were unwrapping her, layer by layer. "Uh, would you like to play one of the video games, Jenny?" she inquired hastily.

"Yes, that would be neat!" The little girl paused. "Is it okay, Daddy?"

"Sure, pumpkin." Without tearing his eyes away from Melinda, he reached into his jeans pocket and pulled out a fistful of quarters. "Have fun."

"I have plenty of change, Mr. Kendall," she assured him in a dignified tone.

His lips twitched. "So what?"

"Your money is not necessary." Melinda's blue eyes flashed.

"Whatever you say, Miss Clarke." Ross suppressed a chuckle. Melinda's unpredictable behavior was causing him no end of astonished delight. In another moment, he half expected her to start spitting at him like an angry kitten. And now, she was even blushing! Ross couldn't quite understand it, but suddenly, something had changed between them. He'd done it, came the triumphant realization. He'd actually succeeded in getting under Melinda Clarke's skin! Silently he watched as she and Jenny ambled over to the video arcade located at the far end of the restaurant. Oh, she probably wasn't even aware of it yet, but to Ross, this startling development opened up an entire new realm of possibilities. Even though she might not be attracted to him, at least he had *some* kind of effect on the delectable Melinda. It was a start, anyhow.

"You must permit me to apologize for Melinda's, er, high-spirited behavior." Peter felt called upon to make some explanation. "I can't imagine what could have gotten into her just before."

Ross waved his hand magnanimously. "Forget it. There's nothing to apologize for, Harrison."

"No?" Peter was clearly relieved.

"In fact, I find your young friend rather... delightful."

"You do?"

Ross watched carefully as the younger man just beamed with pleasure. What a complete idiot! What a dense and utter fool! Only a self-absorbed, egotistical moron like Peter Harrison could have so completely failed to grasp his meaning. Ross intended to use whatever means possible to take his girlfriend away from him. Any way he could. Oh, Melinda probably thought she was in love with the handsome lawyer, but Ross was determined to find a way around *that* minor obstacle. This whole "love" business was entirely overrated, he thought disdainfully.

"I'm so glad you approve of her, Mr. Kendall," Peter admitted. "Frankly, there aren't many women in this town who would make the right kind of wife for someone in my position."

"Wife?" Ross tasted cold steel. "Do you mean to say that the two of you are engaged?"

"Well, I haven't actually asked her yet, but—"

"I'm sure congratulations will soon be in order," came the caustic observation.

"Thanks." Peter paused, then added with pride, "By the way, Melinda happens to be the goddaughter of Arthur Langley."

"Is that a fact?" Ross's response was deceptively bland. In truth, he had never been so perilously close to committing murder. At this very moment, young Harrison had no idea how incredibly lucky he was.

Ross continued to watch as Jenny and Melinda battled alien invaders on the screen of the most popular electronic game in the arcade. The two of them seemed so happy and free from care as their youthful laughter echoed back sweetly in Ross's ears. Melinda *married* to Peter Harrison? The very thought caused an icy anger down his spine. Ross didn't put much credence in hearts and flowers. He certainly had never believed in the sickening sweet sentiment that other people called romance, but if Melinda was going to belong to anyone, it must be to him, and no one else.

"And I'm not a believer in long engagements," Peter confided. "June is a wonderful time for a wedding."

"Is it?" Ross could almost feel his blood boiling. It was taking every ounce of his iron self-control not to grab this smug young puppy by the scruff of the neck and inform him in no uncertain terms that Melinda Clarke was *his* exclusive property. He forced himself to swallow his jealous rage and maintain a calm facade. There wasn't much time left, Ross realized grimly. He would have to move swiftly to disengage Melinda from her blossoming relationship with the marriage-minded Peter Harrison.

"I'd consider it an honor to have you at our wedding, Mr. Kendall."

Ross smiled through gritted teeth. "You're assuming that Miss Clarke is going to say yes."

It was quite obvious that the thought of rejection had never even occurred to Peter. "Oh, she'll say yes," he assured Ross with a bright, confident nod. "I'm sure of it."

Don't count your chickens before they've hatched, buddy boy. The older man concealed the fire in his furious brown eyes. Until now, he had won everything in his life by playing strictly by the rules. By fighting fair and square. But *this* was one battle that would be no-holds-barred. As a shrewd businessman, Ross was already plotting new angles and approaches to the problem. Devising the perfect strategy. He fully intended to enlist Peter Harrison's own conceit and ambition as weapons against him.

With feigned interest, Ross murmured, "On second thought, your proposal for the Humboldt estate might be worthwhile. Perhaps we should discuss it further."

"You want to discuss it?" Peter was unable to hide his elation. "That's just terrific...."

Ross made a pretense of listening while the lawyer droned on and on, but actually he was preoccupied with watching Melinda's golden hair shimmer beneath the fluorescent lighting.

Just then, Jenny apparently scored the winning point in the game, because he could hear her jubilant shout clear across the room. She started to jump up and down in transports of utter delight, as Melinda stood there, with her arms crossed, smiling serenely.

It was at that precise moment, quite unexpectedly, that something warm and wonderful began to melt through the frigid armor of Ross Kendall's cold heart.

Chapter Six

The first in a series of unpleasant surprises happened on the following Monday. The day started out normally enough. It rained on the way to work, and Melinda drove full speed through a giant puddle, splattering mud all over her shiny blue Mustang. When she arrived at her office, she was greeted by the hostile specter of Selene Monroe and her usual heartwarming scowl. Meanwhile, down the hall in the chemistry lab, one of the tenth-graders had accidentally placed the wrong beaker over a Bunsen burner and now the entire building smelled like rotten eggs. So far, a typical morning.

But at lunchtime, she received an exuberant phone call from Peter, informing her that he would have to break all their dates for the next two weeks, but for the most wonderful reason.

"You'll never believe it," he declared ecstatically, "but I have to go to the Caribbean on business!"

"You have to go *where?*"

"There's this tiny, privately owned island in the Caribbean, isn't that incredible? The firm is actually sending *me.*"

"That's wonderful, Peter," Melinda said sincerely, "but I had no idea that Caton and Henderson did much business outside the country."

He laughed. "That's the great part about it. Actually I have Ross Kendall to thank for this opportunity."

"Ross Kendall?" She was suddenly alert.

"See, it pays to do a little networking, right? Apparently he was so impressed by the suggestions I made concerning old Mr. Humboldt's property, that he wants me to research an old land claim for a friend in Venezuela."

"Venezuela?"

Peter sounded almost smug. "Pretty impressive, huh? It seems this business associate of Kendall's is phenomenally rich—real estate, oil, rubber, you name it. Now he's thinking of converting an old sugar plantation into one of those ultra-exclusive resorts. It's on a secluded island about one hundred miles or so off the coast." He paused. "Anyhow, the point is, I'm flying down there tomorrow."

"Oh, I see." Melinda tried to conceal her disappointment. He was pleasant company, and she would certainly miss him during his extended absence. During the past weekend, he'd started to become more affectionate. After bringing her home from their date on Saturday night, he had lingered next to her on the living room couch, his kisses long but gentle. It made Melinda feel a little wistful that just when she was starting to relax and enjoy her relationship with Peter Harrison, he was suddenly being sent out of town for two weeks.

"I hate to hang up, Melinda," he said, a tinge of regret in his voice, "but I've got a million things to do before the end of the day if I'm going to be ready in time."

"I understand," she murmured vaguely. "We can talk later."

"Great. Well, 'bye for now."

After Peter hung up the receiver, Melinda continued to stare at the phone. Why had someone like Ross Kendall done such a great favor for Peter? Last Saturday night, at the pizza parlor, Melinda had gotten the distinct impression that the stern-faced banker hadn't particularly cared for the younger man. She shrugged. Perhaps it was simply her imagination. After all, even if he didn't like Peter very much, since when did personal feelings have anything to do with business? Business was still business to a man like Ross Kendall. Melinda shook her head deprecatingly. Never had she met a man with a more calculating mind. He was certainly a person who would never be ruled by his emotions, there was no doubt whatsoever in her mind about that. The only things that would ever rule Ross Kendall were the mighty case register and a large dose of small-town snobbery.

For three weeks every year, Melinda's parents went on an extended vacation. During that time, the newspapers that carried "Life With Lindy" reprinted the personal favorites selected by the cartoon's creator. This particular Monday marked the first official day of her parent's annual trip abroad, this time to Australia and New Zealand. Unfortunately some of her mother's favorite selections only served to remind Melinda of a time she'd rather forget ever existed. For the past seven years, ever since Melinda had gone off to college and was transformed into a demure adult, Joanna Prescott had kept the mischievous Little Lindy character in a kind of time warp. Millions of readers all over the world seemed to be perfectly content to have Little Lindy remain in high school all these years . . . never to age. Forever a wide-eyed and unpredictable seventeen-year-old. Most of the strips to be reprinted in the next several weeks were at least eight years old and represented events that had actually occurred in Melinda's life. This afternoon in the teacher's lounge, a group of her colleagues were grinning broadly as they passed around the comics section of the daily paper.

"Melinda," asked a smiling Otis Wilkins, the genial head of the history department, "have you read today's *Lindy?*"

"It's a riot," said a grinning Penelope Rourke, the pert gym teacher. "Do you remember that one where Lindy put the box of detergent in the town's public fountain?"

"No, I never read it," Melinda lied smoothly. Oh, of course she remembered pouring an entire carton of laundry soap into the old, ugly fountain on a dare from her brother Devlin. The next morning, there were suds covering the steps of City Hall and all the way down Main Street. The mayor, the chief of police and every merchant in town didn't even have to bother to ask who the perpetrator of the crime was. They all knew it could only be *one* person—Little Lindy Clarke. She'd been nine years old at the time. Now, *that* was a spanking Melinda did not enjoy at all. *Some riot,* she wanted to tell Penelope with a weary sigh.

The next stop was her Fundamentals of Creative Writing class. Lonnie, Brenda and a few of the other girls were already in the classroom, clustered around one of the desks, giggling. "Miss Clarke, have you seen 'Life With Lindy'?" asked Lonnie.

"It's hysterical," chimed in Brenda.

Melinda pressed her lips together tightly. "That's a matter of opinion."

And the day wasn't over yet. Not by a long shot.

Back in her office at the end of the day, Melinda was busily grading essays when Selene burst through the door. Her pinched face was positively ashen.

"Look, Melinda," she asked in an almost beseeching tone, "I've got a parent coming in a few minutes for a conference. Do you suppose you might possibly—"

"Sure, Selene," she finished for her. "I'll clear out and give you some privacy." Obligingly she gathered up the sheaf of papers. "Let me know when you're finished. I'll be in the teachers' lounge."

Almost reluctantly the other woman mumbled a halfhearted "thanks."

Things were looking up, Melinda mused thoughtfully. Selene Monroe was actually being *civil.* Was it perhaps possible that one day the two of them might even become *friends?* Or would that simply be too much to hope for? With a vague half smile, she straightened the collar of her silk blouse and rose from the comfortable seat. Carrying the still-to-be-marked essays in a manila folder tucked securely underneath her arm, Melinda headed toward the door. "See you later," she said to her office-mate and thrust open the heavy wood door. "Oh!"

The tall man Melinda collided with seemed every bit as startled to see her. "Melinda?" exclaimed Ross Kendall as he steadied her briefly with his arms. His tan trench coat was soaked, and so was his close-cropped brown hair. Slender rivulets of water glistened down the sides of his rugged face.

What was he doing here? she wondered fleetingly, then realized that here was Selene Monroe's conference appointment. Was it her imagination, or did he actually seem pleased to see her? "Well, fancy meeting you here," he murmured quietly.

"Yes, well, I believe the person you want to see is my office-mate."

"Your office-mate? Hmm, this is certainly a small world." The slight cynicism in his reply was not lost on Melinda. He seemed to be standing there, waiting for her to say something else. But the last thing she wanted to do at the moment was engage the man in a personal conversation in front of Selene. All she needed now was for the woman to know her personal business.

"I mustn't keep you from your meeting, Mr. Kendall."

"*Mr.* Kendall? Whatever happened to *Ross?*"

Oh, my, Melinda thought now. He really did look devastatingly attractive hovering above her at this moment. In the gloom of the hallway, his scars made him resemble a powerful but weary Roman gladiator. Embarrassed, she forced the romantic image from her mind. What had gotten into her all of a sudden? Since when had she begun poetically comparing ancient warriors to shrewd modern-day businessmen? And why did those incredible brown eyes make her knees turn to jelly? She probably needed her head examined!

Almost as an afterthought, Melinda realized that her silk blouse was moist from the touch of Ross Kendall's rain-drenched hands. "Selene," she murmured nervously, "there's someone here to see you."

"Obviously." The other woman's eyes flickered between them for a brief, curious instant. She extended a perfectly manicured hand. "Mr. Kendall, I'm Selene Monroe, your daughter's teacher."

Ross nodded in curt acknowledgment and stepped into the small room. "Miss Monroe."

Without pausing for an instant, Melinda hastily closed the door behind them and walked purposefully down the hall toward the teachers' lounge.

An hour later, she returned to her office to find Ross Kendall gone and Selene practically in tears. "That has to be absolutely the most pushy, obnoxious man on the face of the earth," she grumbled under her breath.

"Who are you talking about?" Melinda inquired innocently.

"You know very well who I'm talking about—Mr. Ross Kendall! The nerve of that man! Reading me the riot act because he thinks I'm not being sensitive enough to that spoiled little daughter of his!" She paused. "The kid doesn't need sensitivity, she needs a psychiatrist, that's what she needs!"

The last thing Melinda wanted at this moment was a confrontation with her troublesome colleague, but enough was enough. She was utterly fed up with Selene's attitude. "I seriously doubt you have the most remote conception of what a child like Jenny Kendall really needs!"

"*What* did you say?"

"You heard me."

"Just who do you think you are, talking to me like that?" Selene practically hissed.

"I'll tell you who I am," Melinda countered in a quietly dangerous tone. It was a tone she hadn't used since her Little Lindy days. Back then, it had instilled terror in the hearts of her older brothers, who recognized from sad experience that it meant only one thing: *Trouble*. Now Melinda walked around her own desk to face her adversary. "I'll tell you exactly who I am," she repeated. "I'm the person who has to sit here day after day and put up with your nasty attitude and rude remarks. You've gone out of your way to make me feel unwelcome from practically the moment I arrived at Perryville, and made the atmosphere in this cramped office as tense and miserable as possible."

"My, aren't *we* touchy all of a sudden."

"You know what else, Selene? You're a real pain in the butt! Whoever had the bright idea of hiring you to teach little kids ought to have his head examined!''

''I wondered how long it would take you to show your true colors,'' her office-mate sneered.

''Oh, believe me—'' Melinda shook her head slowly ''—I haven't begun to fly my flag yet.''

''It seems to me you've been pretty busy already. However do you manage to dangle *two* men on a string?''

''I haven't the faintest idea what you're talking about.''

The other woman rolled her eyes. ''Give me a break! Just who are you trying to fool with that innocent act of yours? It's not enough you've already got Peter Harrison wrapped around your little finger. I caught the limpid looks you and Ross Kendall exchanged in the doorway!''

''What?'' Melinda stammered.

''Oh, don't bother to deny it. A person had to be deaf not to hear the plaintive tone in the man's voice when he asked you to call him *Ross.*''

''That's none of your business.''

Selene's lips thinned. ''I can certainly understand what you see in the man, that is, if you're willing to stomach that ghastly wreck of a face. Mr. Kendall is one of the richest men in the entire state.''

Melinda felt a flash of white-hot anger. ''I'm going to pretend I didn't hear that.''

''Oh, have I struck a nerve?'' came the unpleasant taunt.

''I warn you, Selene. You're skating on thin ice.''

''Spare me.'' There was a deliberate pause. ''Tell me something else. Whenever did you find the time to whisper all those sweet nothings in Ross Kendall's ear when you were obviously so busy poisoning his mind against me with all that vicious slander?''

Melinda eyed her antagonist levelly. "I never said a word to the man about you. You have my word on that."

"Excuse me if I don't believe you."

"I'll tell you what you can believe, Selene—" she reached for her briefcase and jacket "—any opinion Mr. Ross Kendall has concerning you, rest assured, was earned completely on your own."

"How dare you! Let me warn you—"

"No, let me warn *you,*" Melinda interrupted in a cold voice. "I've tried being nice and I've tried being fair. Neither seems very effective with a person like you, Selene. Obviously threats are the only thing you seem to understand. Very well." She strode toward the door and placed a tense hand on the knob. "I make a better friend than an enemy. Don't try making my life any more difficult than it already is, or—"

"Or *what?*"

There was a sigh. "Let's just say you'll meet a very good friend of mine named *Lindy.*"

"What's that supposed to mean?"

"Forget it." Melinda thrust open the office door and glanced over her shoulder thoughtfully. "Take this bit of friendly advice for what it's worth. If I were you, I'd go out of my way to be a little kinder to students like Jenny Kendall." She turned and left the small room without even waiting to hear Selene Monroe's vitriolic retort.

* * *

The rain was coming down in torrents now, far worse than it had five minutes ago when Melinda had pulled out of the school parking lot. Even with the windshield wipers at full speed, she could barely see the road in front of her. A large van going recklessly fast whizzed by her on a curve and practically sent Melinda careering into a ditch. Just as she was recovering from the sharp swerve, her eyes were diverted by a familiar green car ahead. It was parked along the side of the road at an almost jaunty angle, the hood was up, and the driver hovered over the engine in utter frustration. Apparently Ross Kendall was paying no attention to the heavy sheets of water pelting down over him.

Without a moment's hesitation, Melinda pulled her own mud-splattered vehicle over onto the shoulder and drew the hood of her khaki rain poncho over her head. She emerged from the Mustang and walked briskly toward the disabled Jaguar. It didn't particularly faze her to be in close-enough earshot to hear a succession of angry oaths and colorful epithets being hurled at the expensive automobile by its rather formidable owner. Melinda had grown up in a family of extremely outspoken males.

"What seems to be the trouble?" she inquired mildly.

"Who the—" Ross raised his head and did a double take. "Melinda?"

"I couldn't help but notice a motorist in distress." She tried to sound casual, but something about seeing his strained and weary face was causing strange flutters in her stomach again.

He ran an oil-smeared hand across his rain-soaked forehead, causing a black smear over his tensed eyebrows. "I . . . uh, suppose you heard some rather choice four-letter words just now. Forgive me, but I had no idea anyone else was around."

"Forget it," Melinda said with a mischievous grin. "What is it about mechanical objects that always seems to bring out the beast in a man?"

Ross regarded her silently for a long moment. "I don't seem to have a snappy retort for that one." Abruptly he looked down under the hood again. "To be honest, I haven't the vaguest idea what's wrong with this thing."

"It's a precision machine. You know how temperamental they can be."

"Can they? He rubbed a grimy hand along his hard jaw. "And how much do you know about foreign cars, Miss Melinda Clarke?"

"I'm an ex-tomboy, remember?"

"Do you mean to tell me that in addition to all your other considerable talents, you're also an auto mechanic?"

Melinda crossed her arms with a faint smile. "It doesn't take a qualified mechanic to figure out that you're running on empty, Mr. Ross Kendall."

"I'm *what?*"

She gestured toward the dashboard. "Take a look at the gauge. This fancy British car of yours is simply out of gas."

"That's impossible!" Ross strode heavily to the driver's side and thrust the door open in disbelief. There was an awkward pause. "I don't understand this," came the embarrassed protest. "There must be something wrong with the gauge."

"Mm, right, that must be it."

Ross pulled his lanky, soaking-wet frame out of the Jaguar. "Things like this never happen to me," he uttered in an odd tone.

For the first time, Melinda noticed the thin red streak running along his hairline. "You're bleeding!"

He shrugged indifferently. "It's nothing."

"What do you mean, it's nothing?" She fumbled under the folds of her poncho for a handkerchief. "It's a head injury, isn't it? Now, what happened?"

Melinda's sudden display of concern left Ross at a complete loss. "It's no big deal...." he murmured slowly. "I grazed my head on the hood, that's all."

But it wasn't all, not to Melinda. All at once, something had stirred within her, seeing this vital, proud man grimy, bedraggled and soaked to the skin. The blood on his haggard face merely served to intensify Melinda's instinctive need to soothe and nurture. At this moment, Ross Kendall seemed more like a proud, injured panther than a man.

Without a moment's hesitation, she stepped up against him and began to gently dab at the cut with the clean square of embroidered linen.

"What...what are you doing?" he stared down at her with a slight tremor.

"What does it look like?" She pulled back with an impatient gesture. "No, this isn't any good. I can't clean the cut adequately out here. I'll need some hydrogen peroxide. That's all right, I've got some in the medicine cabinet." With a light touch on his arm, she pointed toward her own car. "Come on, I'll drive you."

"You'll drive me where?" Ross stilled her hand on his drenched sleeve.

"Well, we can't very well take your car, can we? Come on now, you're probably going to catch pneumonia at this rate."

He seemed utterly dazed. "Where are we going?"

"Back to my place."

"*Your* place!"

Melinda shrugged. "Of course. It's a lot closer than yours."

"Oh." Had a land mine been detonated under his feet at this very instant, Ross could not have been more stunned.

"We can lock up your car and come back with gasoline a little later."

Ross nodded mutely. Bemused, he allowed himself to be led to Melinda's car. A few minutes later, they were pulling into the parking stall at the small garden apartment complex. After a slight hesitation, he remarked, "You know, I believe you might be right."

Melinda shut off the engine. "Right about what?"

"My head." Ross gave his best imitation of a wince. "It's really starting to ache."

"Oh!" she exclaimed in alarm. "Let's get you inside at once."

"That's a good idea," he agreed weakly. "Do you have any aspirin in that medicine cabinet of yours?"

"I have everything you could possibly need," she said in her most assuring, motherlike tone.

"I don't doubt it," Ross murmured under his breath. But Melinda didn't hear the remark. She was already out of the Mustang and coming around the other side to assist her very willing patient.

Chapter Seven

While Ross removed his sodden raincoat and stood strangely silent in the living room, Melinda quickly retrieved the necessary items from the bathroom cabinet. The thought raced through her mind that after all these months, Ross Kendall was only the second guest she had ever entertained in this apartment. *Entertained?* No, Melinda corrected herself hastily. That was not the reason she had brought home this rather unexpected guest. She was merely being a Good Samaritan, that was all. Well, in any event, thank goodness the place was neat and freshly dusted! Emerging from the bedroom, she was struck by the way her tall, powerfully built visitor seemed to dwarf the tiny living room. Ross Kendall against the distinctly feminine backdrop of lacy white French curtains and fluffy patchwork cushions appeared rather ill-at-ease.

"I don't mean to put you to any trouble." His tone was uncomfortably polite.

"It's no trouble." Melinda gestured at the old-fashioned faded blue velvet armchair. "Just sit down there, and I'll get you a glass of water for these aspirins."

Silently Ross waited as Melinda poured some water from the tap into an empty jelly glass illustrated with cartoon animals. Somewhat apologetically, she handed him the water. "I hope you're impressed. I'm using my best crystal."

His lips twitched. "I'm touched, Melinda."

"I just knew you would be." Melinda felt suddenly lighthearted. "Now, let me take care of that forehead." Gingerly, with a moist washcloth, she began to dab away the dirt and grease from his face in preparation for applying the antiseptic. She worked gently and efficiently, so absorbed in her task that two things failed to occur to her. The first was the fact that the skin she was touching was horribly scarred. The second was the inescapable fact that to tend to her patient, Melinda had to lean up against the armchair, her slender body practically touching his. She was scarcely aware that Ross's breath had caught in his throat as her soft, scented warmth pressed nearer to his. "This will sting for a second," Melinda warned as she dabbed the cotton ball soaked with peroxide onto the thin, jagged cut.

Ross flinched, but he wasn't in pain. To him, this was the most unbearably sweet torture—having Melinda so close. Her parted lips hovered barely an inch from his own, and for a shattering instant, her breasts brushed against his shoulder. Involuntarily Ross stiffened.

"Have I hurt you?" Melinda asked in alarm.

"No, of course not," he uttered raggedly.

It was then, somewhat belatedly, that she realized how intimate their positions really were—practically an embrace. Her fingertips rested comfortably along the lapel of his fine wool suit, and the open vee of her silk blouse almost cradled Ross Kendall's astounded jaw. "Oh, excuse me." She started to pull back in embarrassment, only to feel a pair of firm hands grasp both sides of her waist.

"Excuse what?" came the hoarse taunt.

"I . . . I shouldn't be—"

His eyes darkened. "Oh, yes! Oh, yes, you *should,* honey. Come here!" In a single, sweeping motion, Ross pulled her down into his lap. And then his hard mouth claimed hers in an urgent, hungry kiss.

It was a kiss that brooked no refusals, a kiss that sought to claim all that had been previously denied. Melinda struggled only briefly against the shocking electric contact. Ross tasted of tobacco and peppermint, and the sensual musky scent of his after-shave had an allure of its own. Against her own volition, she began to savor this exquisite assault on her senses. Melinda now relaxed in his arms and yielded at last to the maddeningly sweet pleasure only this man's lips could give her.

This unexpectedly willing surrender astonished him. "Melinda!" Ross stared down at her, an alien glitter in his eyes.

"What?" she breathed softly in a voice that wasn't her own.

He shook his head in disbelief. "You really know how to knock a man's socks off, don't you?"

"I wouldn't know." Her eyes lowered. "I've never knocked anyone's socks off before."

"Well, trust me," came the unsteady response, "you most certainly have *now.*"

Melinda just gazed up at him incredulously. His muscular body was tense and almost trembling. Was it possible she could actually affect a man this way? It gave her the most delicious feeling of feminine power. "I suppose this sort of thing must happen to you all the time." Her voice quivered.

"Is that what you really think?" His brown gaze darkened. "That I go around kissing every woman I can get my hands on?"

"Don't you?"

A gentle fingertip traced the delicate line of her cheek. "Why are you always ready to believe the worst about me?" Ross mused in a bittersweet tone.

"I never said—"

That fingertip stilled the protest on her lips. "It doesn't matter. Just as long as you kiss me again, Melinda!" He groaned and pulled her roughly against him once more. This time, his mouth was more possessive and demanding.

All further protests banished from her mind, Melinda allowed herself to be swept away by this second dizzying embrace. Throwing caution to the wind, she pressed her soft body against his hard strength and wound her arms around his neck. She lost all sense of time and place in the wonderment of discovery. So *this* was the way it could feel, Melinda marveled. Hot. Burning. Out of control. It was reckless and yet at the same time, so utterly right. Under the increased pressure of his hard mouth, she parted her lips to allow an even more intimate kiss. Ross's tongue stabbed sharply into her warm, inner moistness—probing, tasting and laying claim to all that was his.

"You're so sweet," he practically rasped, "so unbelievably sweet!" His hand smoothed the loose blond wisps back from her forehead. "And your hair is like silk...."

Melinda gave an involuntary shudder as his fingers teased the bare skin of her nape. "Ross!"

His eyes twinkled. "If kissing you is all it takes to get back on a first-name basis, I ought to do it more often." He seemed ten years younger all of a sudden, the lines of weariness completely gone from his face. Sure hands gently stroked the straight line of her back. "But why am I wasting time talking?" As his hard lips descended toward her waiting mouth yet again, Melinda felt like a drowning swimmer going under for the last time.

Just as Ross's tongue renewed its hungry exploration of her mouth, something else began to happen. She could feel one of his hands slowly moving toward the front of her thin blouse. "No, don't!" Melinda gave a stunned whisper and stilled his bold fingers just as they reached the side of one breast.

"Don't what?" he uttered thickly.

"Touch me like that," she exclaimed in a soft, breathless voice.

"But I want to touch you there. I want to touch you everywhere, honey." He stared down at her through hooded eyes. "Does that shock you?"

Yes, it shocks me, Melinda wanted to cry out. *It shocks me because I want it, too!* He was utterly the wrong man for her. He was wrong in every way imaginable. And she had better stop this madness before she was too far in over her head. The vital warmth of his athletic body through the expensive suit fabric was exhilarating and disturbing at the same time. Ross Kendall was way too sophisticated for Melinda's peace of mind. His subtle brand of seduction was beyond her woefully inadequate experience.

Ross smiled knowingly and cupped her face between his hands. "Listen to me, Melinda—"

But before he could finish what he was about to say, the moment was shattered by the piercing buzz of the doorbell. Melinda fought the deep, delicious languor that threatened to overwhelm any further attempts at resistance. "I have to answer that!" she exclaimed hastily.

Ross gave a heavy sigh. "No, you don't."

"Yes, I do," came the insistent reply. Briefly Melinda struggled to free herself from her compromising position in his lap. The doorbell continued to ring in a loud staccato.

"Are you in there?" Peter's curious voice filtered through the wooden front door.

"Just a minute!" she called out shakily.

"Right," Ross said tautly and released his possessive grasp. "It's almost time for a sentimental farewell with loverboy. Tell me, have you two set the date yet?"

Melinda stared at him. "What are you talking about?"

"The wedding."

She scrambled out of the chair. "Why are you speaking like this?"

He laughed mirthlessly. "It's all right, Melinda. You don't have to pretend with me."

"Pretend *what?*" The doorbell continued to buzz, unanswered. She was deaf to everything except the sudden note of harsh cynicism in Ross's voice. Was this tight-mouthed man the same person who had just moments before whispered the most passionate urgings against her flushed cheeks?

"Oh, go ahead," he grated out, "answer the damn door for all I care!"

Numbly she made her way across the living room rug toward the door and passed the hall mirror. She paused to regard her disheveled appearance. Quickly Melinda straightened her skirt and tucked in the tails of her silk blouse. She then ran a nervous hand over her loosened wisps of hair. But there was no concealing the brightness in her blue eyes, and her lips remained slightly swollen and tender from Ross Kendall's heated kisses.

"Melinda—" Peter began to sound annoyed. "I'm kind of in a hurry, hon!"

"Just a second," came the almost irritable mutter. She forced a smile and thrust open the front door.

Peter stood there in his pin-striped blue suit, with a broad grin and holding a bouquet of yellow roses. "I was wondering if you were ever going to answer the buzzer!" He kissed her briefly on the lips and handed her the flowers.

"Thank you," Melinda murmured. "They're lovely."

He winked cheerfully. "Nothing's too good for my girl." She could feel Ross Kendall's eyes burning into her back like two red-hot coals as Peter stepped jauntily into the small apartment. *I'm not your girl!* Melinda wanted to shout out loud... *I'm not anybody's girl.* She gave a weary sigh. *Men!*

"Anyhow, I still have a zillion things to attend to before tomorrow, but I really wanted to come over and say goodbye, well, *properly.*" He ran a nervous hand through his perfectly styled blond hair. "That is, uh, since I'm leaving for two entire weeks, it might be a good idea to ask you now and make it official."

She eyed him warily. "Make what official?"

Peter reached into his trousers pocket, only to be startled by a harsh cough from the direction of the living room. Up until that moment he had been completely unaware of the tall, unsmiling man whose presence was obscured by the winged armchair facing in the other direction. "Mr. Kendall?" he declared in astonishment.

"Hello, there, Harrison."

Peter seemed perplexed but pleased. "Imagine running into you here, of all places."

"Yes, it's a small world." There was a faint trace of sarcasm in Ross's words, but obviously Peter was once again unaware of the tension in the small room.

Melinda didn't feel much like making any explanations. Besides, what could she say that wouldn't be either a lie or just plain embarrassing? Finally she compromised. "Ross.... I mean, Mr. Kendall's car broke down, and I gave him a ride back here."

Ross twisted his mouth. "Yes, that's right."

Peter shook his head sympathetically. "Hey, that's a shame. Anything I can do to help?"

There was an uncomfortable silence. "Actually Melinda was kind enough to let me make a phone call to the service station."

Melinda met his cool gaze head on. "Yes, did you find that listing in the phone book yet?"

His eyes darkened. "No, I'm still looking." He crossed his arms in a thoughtful pose. "It just occurred to me that it's your last evening in Perryville for a long time, Harrison. You and Melinda here probably want a little privacy. I feel simply terrible having to ask you this favor...."

"What favor?" Peter's face lit up eagerly.

Melinda raised an eyebrow. "Yes, *what* favor?"

Ross strolled over to retrieve his sodden trench coat where it lay across a vinyl kitchen chair. He rubbed his angular jaw pensively. "I was hoping I could prevail upon you to give me a ride to the nearest gas station. You see, the truth of the matter is, I have a, um, broken fuel gauge. As it develops, what I really need is a gallon of gasoline to start the engine."

The ambitious young lawyer was delighted at this unexpected opportunity to ingratiate himself with his prestigious client. "No trouble at all, Mr. Kendall. I'd be pleased to help in any way I can." He pulled his hand out of trouser pocket. Whatever small package he had been about to remove and whatever urgent question he had been planning to ask of Melinda, had both been quickly forgotten in the face of Mr. Ross Kendall and his casual request. After all, Peter had his priorities.

"That's very decent of you, Harrison. I really appreciate it." He made a point of checking his wristwatch with a mild degree of impatience. "Of course, I hate to rush you, but—"

"Oh, no problem!" Peter assured him with an almost obsequious air that rather annoyed Melinda. "And by the way, Mr. Kendall, let me take this opportunity to thank you for recommending me to your Venezuelan contacts."

"Think nothing of it," came the enigmatic reply. "I'd like to see you get everything you deserve."

"Thank you very much, sir!" Peter actually preened. He tuned to Melinda with an almost proud smile. "I'll try to make it back a little later, if I can take care of everything else. You understand, don't you, hon?"

Why wasn't she even the slightest bit disappointed? she wondered. "Sure, I understand."

"Excuse me while I kiss my best girl goodbye," Peter murmured to Ross almost apologetically.

"By all means." There was the slightest hint of mild sarcasm in the older man's voice. "You go right ahead and just kiss Melinda goodbye." But his expression remained unreadable as he watched Peter tenderly draw her into his arms and touch her lips in a gentle but lingering caress.

Melinda was the first to pull away. "Have a wonderful trip," she said sincerely. But all she could think of now was the tingling effect of Ross Kendall's kisses just a few moments before. In contrast, Peter's embrace had left her, as always, completely unmoved. What made it all so downright awkward was the disturbing presence of Ross as a one-man audience to

Peter's possessive farewell kiss. Despite the bland demeanor on the banker's face, Melinda was quite convinced he was watching her with utter disdain. To her complete chagrin, she suddenly realized that it *did* matter what Ross Kendall thought. She honestly cared that his opinion of her be a positive one. Oh, this was awful...no, disastrous! It went further than Melinda had previously feared. What she really wanted was for Ross to *like* her.

"I tell you, Mr. Kendall," Peter gave a cocky smile. "I'm going to miss this girl when I'm gone. She's one in a million."

Ross stared at Melinda strangely. "I'm inclined to agree."

"Yes, I'm a lucky guy." The handsome young attorney placed a proprietary arm around her waist, pausing to bestow a brief peck on the cheek. "I'll call you later on, hon."

"All right."

Neither of them noticed the dark shadow that flickered across Ross's hard face. "Goodbye, Melinda," he said in a curt, emotionless tone. "Thank you for the use of your telephone."

Her throat felt dry. "You're welcome, Mr. Kendall." With a hollow sensation in her stomach, she watched as both men walked out the door and into the pelting rain.

Later on that evening, she received a somewhat apologetic phone call from Peter, explaining why he couldn't stop by, after all. "Ross Kendall had some papers involving his daughter's trust fund that he needed some last-minute advice on, and somehow, they'd gotten misplaced. By the time we tracked them down, it was almost dinnertime, and he invited me to stay for the meal." Peter paused. "I could hardly say no."

"Oh, certainly not." Melinda rolled her eyes and stared up at the ceiling.

"Listen, I want to ask you a favor. It seems like our Mr. Kendall might want to start using my legal services on a more regular basis. Isn't that the most terrific news?"

Something didn't sound quite right, but she merely said, "Yes, that sounds great. I'm very happy for you, Peter."

"Anyhow, the thing is, you know that old expression, 'out of sight, out of mind'? Well, if I can't be in town for the next couple of weeks, somebody else in the firm might seize the opportunity to rack up a few brownie points with Kendall, and where would that leave me?" Peter's tone was beguiling. "I got the idea during dinner at his house tonight. That little kid, what's-her-name—"

"Jenny."

"Whatever. All she could talk about was what a great person you were. The whole meal, it was 'Miss Clarke this' and 'Miss Clarke that,' get the picture?"

"No."

"Sure you do. The little girl loves you. Ross Kendall loves his little girl. Spend some time with them."

Melinda clenched the receiver tightly. "What?"

"Oh, c'mon, I'd really appreciate it."

Her tone grew frigid. "I don't think—"

"Look, I know it sounds like a major bore, but being a little nice to the Kendalls could earn *us* some serious brownie points."

Peter's mercenary attitude was starting to annoy Melinda more and more. "What makes you think I'd care in the slightest about so-called brownie points?"

He hesitated sheepishly. "Well, I thought we could discuss it when I returned from the Caribbean. I guarantee the answer will please you."

This only increased her puzzlement. "I simply don't believe in being nice to people for ulterior motives. Don't ever ask me to do it again, Peter."

The voice on the other line was clearly uncomfortable. "Then I suppose you aren't going to like what I did."

A warning bell went off in her head. "What did you do?"

"I was really clever about it, Melinda. I told Mr. Kendall how terrible I felt about leaving you alone for two entire weeks, and how you were still relatively new in town and didn't know very many people outside of school."

"Oh, *honestly!*"

"Well, it's true, isn't it?"

Melinda was exasperated. "That's not the point!"

"No, I suppose not." He sighed. "Well I guess you'd better hear the worst of it."

"Do you mean, it gets *worse?*"

"Ross...that is, Mr. Kendall, said that seeing as my trip to the Caribbean is indirectly his fault, he feels, well, obligated to keep an eye on you during my absence."

Melinda was mortified. "He feels obligated?"

"Darn nice of the man, wouldn't you say?"

"That's not quite how I'd put it," she said through her teeth. *Obligated?* Was that how Ross Kendall felt? What was she, anyhow? Some kind of charity case?

"So, don't be surprised if he calls you sometime this week and invites you over for dinner or out to a movie."

"Well, he can just forget it!"

Peter was alarmed. "You can't mean that."

"Oh, yes I do."

"Please, Melinda! I can't afford to alienate such an important client." He sounded utterly miserable. "I'm sorry that I didn't consult you first."

"Hmm!"

"I guess I was so excited about everything, I just didn't stop to consider your feelings." There was an awkward pause. "If he does call, please reconsider, won't you? How boring could an evening with Ross Kendall be, anyway?"

"All right." Melinda simply gave in. She was just tired with discussing the matter. And if she knew Peter, he wouldn't stop harping on it until she yielded at last. It had taken the past few days for it to finally hit her that Peter Harrison wasn't quite the man she had been searching for. Beneath the handsome, boyish package was a person who was rather self-centered and devoid of true depth. She decided reluctantly that when the young attorney returned from the Caribbean, it might be best if the two of them didn't see each other quite as much as before.

"So, you'll go out with Ross Kendall if he calls you?" Peter was triumphant.

"Yes," she sighed unhappily. "*If* he calls me."

* * *

It was nearly eleven o'clock when the phone rang again. This time it was Ross Kendall. "I realize it's a bit late," he began slowly, "but would you like to have dinner tomorrow?"

"Dinner?" Melinda murmured as if she'd never heard of the word.

There was an awkward pause. "Yes, *dinner.* It's a meal people usually have at the end of a long, hard day."

Of course she wanted to have dinner with Ross Kendall and his daughter, Jenny. But Melinda's pride kept harking back to Peter's words. *He feels obligated.* "Why are you asking me?" The words spilled out almost accusingly.

"Why, indeed?" Ross's tone was ironic.

"I know what you told Peter." There was an icy note in her voice. "Please don't feel obligated in any way."

"Obligated?" He sounded incredulous. "What on earth are you talking about?"

"Forget it."

"But I don't want to forget it. Let me make this very clear, Melinda. I *want* to have dinner with you."

She sighed. "All right."

"Good." He sounded smugly satisfied. "I'll pick you up at six."

"But I thought—"

"You thought what?"

Melinda felt caught in an elaborate web. What could she say to Ross? That she had blindly assumed that the invitation was for a homey dinner at the

Kendall house? This was beginning to sound suspiciously like a date.

"Why so silent?" Ross inquired thinly. "Are you having second thoughts?"

Who was she kidding? Melinda asked herself. Whether he was motivated by obligation or something else, the truth was she wanted to spend more time with Ross. Despite all the danger signs looming over the horizon, despite his utter unsuitability, he was the one man she simply could not resist. Why fight it?

Chapter Eight

Melinda was determined not to make a fuss over her appearance tonight. It was just fine with her if Ross Kendall believed she was indifferent to the prospect of an evening in his company. In truth, the idea of several hours alone with the man was wreaking havoc on her normally unflappable nerves. Melinda assured herself that the only reason she raced home from school in time to take a luxurious scented bubble bath was because she needed to relax after a long day. And if she took extra pains to wash and blow-dry her hair so that it fell past her shoulders in loose, glossy waves it was because wearing it in a tight French braid sometimes gave her a headache. And last but not least, the only reason she changed from ultra-casual slacks at the last minute into an exceedingly feminine, figure-flattering pink sweater dress was because the slacks were wrinkled.

The doorbell rang promptly at six. When she opened the door he just stood there for a moment and stared at her. "You look beautiful," Ross uttered simply, unable to take his eyes away.

"Thank you," she managed finally. "You look very nice yourself."

He twisted his hard lips. "It's not necessary to compliment me in return, Melinda. I know very well just how I look."

Anger rose inside her. "Obviously not." Didn't the man have any conception of how devastatingly attractive he was this evening? In a soft wheat-colored cotton shirt, beige slacks and a supple chocolate-brown leather jacket, Ross was casually elegant, exuding his distinctive brand of male allure from every pore of his six-foot-two frame.

Something flickered in his eyes for a moment. "Are you saying that you *like* the way I look?"

"Yes."

Ross shook his head in wonderment. "There's no end to your surprises, is there, honey?" Bending over, he caught her lips in a brief, shattering kiss. Just as before, he tasted of tobacco and mint. "But then, everything about you is a sweet surprise, Melinda."

Without waiting for her astonished reply, he led her downstairs to his waiting car.

As she quietly sat back against the comfortable leather seat, it seemed as if a dozen butterflies fluttered in Melinda's stomach. How was it possible to feel so utterly comfortable and nervous at the same time? Ross's brief kiss still tingled on her lips, a tantalizing promise of what was yet to come. She stole a glance at Ross's hard profile as he concentrated on the road ahead. Melinda had been inexperienced, even shy, when it came to sexual matters—but she most certainly was not naive. Like millions of other women out for an evening with an attractive and exciting man, the thoughts racing through her mind right now were no different. How would the evening end? Would he try to make love to her? And if so, did she truly want to resist such an overture? Melinda had waited almost twenty-five years for the exquisite intimacy only a man could give her, yet in the short space of one week, all her sturdy barriers were crumbling under the expert assault of Ross Kendall. There was no logic, she couldn't explain it even if she wanted to.

At that moment, Ross turned his eyes fleetingly from the wooded country highway and smiled. It broke the tension in his harsh features and caused a surge of warmth throughout Melinda's body. She smiled back and shrugged away any more disturbing thoughts. Who cared about logic or explanations? Since when did love make any sense?

Love? No, that couldn't be possible! Melinda scrambled to recover from the shocking emotional blow. No, she argued futilely with herself, it wasn't supposed to happen this way. Love was a delicate, fragile entity, wasn't it? Love was supposed to grow slowly and then come into glorious flower under a moonlit sky, or during a romantic tropical sunset. Since when did any person in her right mind realize she was in love while riding in an automobile?

"Is something wrong?" Ross asked suddenly, the tension back in his voice.

"No, not at all!" she answered hastily, her red flush of mortification unnoticed in the dark car.

It was his own fault, Ross thought with a heavy sigh. He'd practically coerced Melinda into coming along on this date in the first place, and now he couldn't even hold up his own end of the conversation. He had been so confident, so sure of himself, until now. He had been so smugly convinced of his cleverness in eliminating Peter Harrison from the scene for the next two precious weeks. His old friend Miguel Santerra had been of inestimable assistance in that quarter. He'd make sure that the smug young attorney would be bogged down for at least that long searching through dusty deeds and old documents.

Meanwhile, that would leave Ross free to win Melinda for himself.

Yesterday afternoon had been dangerously close. When he had seen Harrison reaching into his pocket, it was obvious he had been about to remove an engagement ring. Before Peter's arrival had shattered their own delightful tête-à-tête, however, Ross had caught a delicious glimpse of the possibility that Melinda could be his. Holding Melinda in his arms had been such a sweet pleasure. Her willing response had nearly driven him to lose control. Ross's hands tightened on the leather-covered steering wheel. Getting ready for tonight, he'd been as nervous as a teenager on his first date. But that's how Melinda made him feel. New. Undamaged. Full of hope and dreams. But how could he possibly believe that, after a lifetime of rejection, someone as lovely and desirable as Melinda Clarke could actually *want* him? That took quite a leap of faith, and faith was something that Ross Kendall had only ever possessed in severely short supply.

He glanced at Melinda again. With her hair hanging gloriously loose against the soft pink curves of that delectably clinging confection of a dress, it was taking every ounce of willpower he possessed not to pull the car off the road this very minute and take her into his arms.

Ross struggled for composure. "Jenny sends her regards. She seems to be getting on a little better in class."

"I'm glad. Jenny is such a sweet little girl."

"Well, you've made a difference, believe me." Ross hesitated. "It hasn't been easy for my daughter. Even though she's made it clear that she prefers living with me over her mother, she still misses her old school terribly."

Melinda regarded him with compassion. "It'll take time, Ross, but believe me, she'll adjust. Life is never easy, especially when you're only ten years old."

"Except in your case. I understand you owned the world at the age of ten."

She shook her head. "That was different."

"I don't doubt it. How many people can say they've had a childhood like Little Lindy's?" He paused again. "I'd give anything to see Jenny get into a little healthy mischief."

"Be careful what you wish for," Melinda quoted the old expression warningly. "You just might get it."

Ross's eyes glimmered. "I certainly hope so," he murmured softly. "I certainly hope so." But he wasn't talking about Jenny.

*   *   *

The Green Chimney was a rustic country inn built from an eighteenth-century farmhouse of weathered brick and stone. It was located nearly twenty miles away in the small town of Henfield. This peaceful dairy town was known for its quaint old buildings and serene landscape, and had become the secret weekend and summer getaway for wealthy city dwellers. When Ross's Jaguar pulled into the gated entrance and he handed his keys to the red-jacketed parking valet, Melinda just stared at the elegant building. "We're eating *here?*"

Ross looked at her quietly. "Is it all right? If you'd rather go somewhere else—"

"No, it's lovely," she stammered. The Green Chimney was considered to be amongst the most posh restaurants in the country. Already, she could see other arrivals in expensive furs and diamonds. It was almost like a scene out of that trendy television program that profiled favorite haunts of the chic and wealthy. Thank goodness she had decided not to wear her old slacks and a sweater. Was this the place Ross Kendall always took his dates to? For the first time in her life, Melinda experienced a sudden, jolting jealousy. It was not a particularly pleasant sensation.

But thoughts of Ross and the other women in his life quickly evaporated in the heady delight of the evening. At a secluded table by a fireplace, they shared a bottle of Chablis, dined on a light seafood mousse, followed by sliced veal in a delicate lemon-chive sauce. Maybe it was the several glasses of wine that made Melinda relax, or perhaps she had just needed the extra dose of courage, but finally, she looked across the table in the candlelight and asked, "Do you come here often?"

"No." He stared at her for a long moment. "I've never even been here before."

"Oh." She tried to hide her surprise.

"What did you think, Melinda? That I come here all the time, as part of my free-wheeling, glittering social life?" There was no doubting the mild sarcasm in his voice.

But Melinda was struggling with new feelings and more than a little bit of wine. "Yes," she responded simply, "that's just what I think."

He reached across the table and grasped her hand. "How little you really know me." How could he explain to the owner of those two startled blue eyes exactly how lonely his life had been all these years without appearing pathetic?

"I want to know you, Ross." The words were out before she could stop herself. "I want to know you better."

His hard fingers tightened on hers. "Don't play with me, Melinda. I couldn't stand it if you did."

I could never do that, she answered silently. *How could I when I'm in love with you, Ross Kendall?* But she just returned his solemn stare and said with artificial lightness, "You seem to know a great deal about me, but what do I really know about you?"

He released her hand abruptly. "There isn't very much to know."

With a boldness Melinda didn't realize she possessed, she burst out the question. "It's none of my business, but tell me about Jenny's mother."

A pained expression darkened his face, and she was immediately sorry for asking. "Of course it's your business," he corrected her quietly. "But there really isn't much to tell."

Ross fought to find the right words to tell Melinda about the cold ruthlessness of the woman he had been foolish enough to marry. How could he explain that as a callow, unattractive twenty-four-year-old he had been dazzled by Deirdre's dark, sultry beauty, only to face a rude awakening after the wedding? That she had deliberately sought him out for his family's wealth and prestige, and her social-climbing, manipulative parents had encouraged that match. How could he admit to Melinda that his wife had never loved him, never even cared a little for him? After the birth of their daughter she had flaunted her numerous other lovers defiantly in his face and dared him to divorce her. But Ross's stubborn pride refused to admit his marriage had been a sham and a failure from the start. The only thing that had made the entire charade worthwhile had been Jenny.

"Forget I said anything." Melinda now glanced across the table apprehensively. "I should never have asked."

"No," Ross fidgeted briefly with a cigarette before striking a match to the tip. "I'll tell you about Deirdre." There was a bitterness to his tone that she had never heard before. "But I'll do us both a favor and make a long story short." He took a deep drag of the cigarette and forced himself to continue. "My wife married me for my money and the promise of a glamorous life-style."

His voice was hard as he continued. "She hated Perryville and never stopped insisting that we move to London or Paris. We fought about it all the time. Until that *last* time." Ross's voice drifted off. Even now it was an ugly, searing memory. Driving home in the rain. That final terrible argument. Skidding off the slick, wet highway. Shattered glass and shards of twisted metal. Mind-numbing pain. He tried to sound matter-of-fact. "There was an accident one night. I went through the windshield and got *this*." He gestured at his cheek. Never mind the broken bones, he thought bitterly. The injury to his face would last forever.

Melinda's heart was overwhelmed with love and compassion. She ached for the pain Ross had suffered and wanted nothing more at this moment than to take him in her arms and hold him until the hurt subsided. How could she have ever believed the man to be cold and unfeeling? But all she could say aloud was a tremulous, "I'm so sorry."

He grimaced. "You don't have to be. It happened a long time ago, and I've gotten used to it." He briefly touched the jagged strip of scars covering one side of his gaunt face. "I don't want your pity, Melinda!" Ross crushed out the cigarette in the ashtray with a harsh motion.

"And what exactly *do* you want?" Her own voice shook.

"Do you really want me to answer that?" came the hoarse reply.

But before Melinda could nod a mute assent, the moment was shattered by the reappearance of their waiter bringing coffee and dessert. Almost with relief, Ross immediately changed the subject. "So tell me," he asked with deliberate lightness, "have you heard anything from Harrison?"

She raised an eyebrow. "No."

"You mean to tell me he didn't call his 'best girl' yet to let her know that he'd arrived safely?"

"No."

His expression was odd. "Now, why do I get the distinct impression that you don't want to talk about your handsome lawyer?"

"He isn't *my* lawyer!" Why was he baiting her this way? Just a few brief moments ago, Melinda had come so tantalizingly close to the *real* Ross Kendall. This was utterly exasperating!

"Really?" There was a hard edge to his voice as he pulled out a gold pen and signed the restaurant check. "What would you call him, then?"

"For heaven's sake!" Melinda's eyes blazed. "Why are you asking me this?"

He snapped the cap back onto the elegant pen and roughly shoved it back inside his jacket pocket. "I thought that was obvious."

"Well, excuse me for not being a mind reader!"

Ross coolly studied her flushed, angry face. "All right, then. Tell me something. If Peter Harrison were still in Perryville and not the Caribbean, would you still have gone out to dinner with me tonight?"

Melinda returned the challenge. "Would you still have asked me?"

He gave a faint smile. "Don't you already know the answer?"

"I already told you, I'm not a mind reader."

"So I'm beginning to realize," came the dry observation.

The rest of the conversation was somewhat stilted and bland. Ross discussed interesting historical facts about Perryville, when all Melinda really wanted to know was how he felt about *her*. He asked Melinda polite questions about her childhood as Little Lindy, but all Melinda could think of was how much she wanted to run her fingers through his short brown hair. How had it come to this? she wondered irritably. Never in her life had she ever felt so emotionally charged over a man. And how was it possible to feel such an irrevocable physical link and not have the other person be aware of it?

"And speaking of your colleague, I'm sure Miss Monroe told you that I hardly approve of her teaching methods," Ross was saying now.

Damn that Selene, she groaned inwardly. *Leave it to her to show up everywhere, like the proverbial bad penny!* But aloud, Melinda merely gave a nod. "Yes, she certainly made her opinion known to me."

Ross shook his head in annoyance. "Frankly I find her to be temperamentally unsuitable to teach younger children, but what's the point of kicking up a fuss when there are only a few weeks left in the semester?" There was a pause. "Besides, I couldn't get the woman fired even if I wanted to."

"Why not?" It sounded like an excellent idea to Melinda. Selene Monroe simply didn't belong teaching the lower grades. Melinda had a kind heart, but she had absolutely no sympathy for adults who made the learning process an unpleasant one.

Ross seemed surprised at Melinda's harsh attitude toward her colleague, but made no further comment other than, "You know, of course, that Miss Monroe's aunt is a member of the academy's board of trustees."

"No, I didn't." Well, she thought cynically, that explained everything. *Typical.*

Ross eyed her curiously. "I take it that there's no love lost between the two of you."

"That's an understatement."

"I can understand her feelings all too well."

Melinda drew herself up stiffly in her chair. "And what is that supposed to mean?"

He stifled a nervous laugh. "Don't misunderstand. What I meant was, oh hell, I didn't mean that I agreed with the little shrew!"

But the damage had already been done. "What *did* you mean, then?"

Ross was totally mortified by the hurt expression on Melinda's lovely face. Leave it to him to somehow manage to say something incredibly dumb and heavy-handed at just the wrong moment! "What I meant to say was that your office-mate has every reason to resent you."

"Oh, thank you. *That's* even better," came the icy reply.

"What I'm trying to tell you is that someone as beautiful as you would make any woman jealous."

Something warm flickered in Melinda's heart for a moment, but the contrary imp that controlled her pride had a mind of its own. Dealing with the vulnerability her newly discovered feelings for Ross had caused made Melinda want to lash out with a little green-eyed monster of her own. "That's kind of you to say, Ross." She forced an amused smile. "I agree that Selene Monroe is jealous of me, but the reason is far more practical than the one you mention." She noted her companion's quirked eyebrow and forged recklessly ahead. "The answer is two little words— Peter Harrison."

The glare Ross gave her could have scorched the room. "Peter Harrison?" he practically rasped.

"She's got quite a crush on the man, and naturally she's jealous."

"Naturally," came the dull echo. "Well, I wouldn't worry." He smiled back through clenched teeth. "Miss Monroe doesn't stand a chance against the competition. You and loverboy can live happily ever after."

"What on earth are you talking about?"

His reply was bitter. "Do I have to spell it out, Melinda? You can have any man you want."

She shook her head. "Apparently not." *I can't have you, Ross Kendall.* It was a wearying, defeated thought. All she wanted to do was go home.

Ross stared at her grimly. "And what is that supposed to mean?"

"It means—" Melinda took a deliberate glance at her silver wristwatch "—it's getting late, and I've got a long day tomorrow."

His eyes darkened. "Of course. I was about to suggest the same thing." He stood up abruptly. "It's time we were leaving."

How had it suddenly happened? Melinda thought with a strange ache as they drove home in silence. How had a pleasant evening deteriorated into such an uncomfortable situation? She leaned back in the Jaguar, puzzled and confused. How could everything end on such a flat, disappointing note? Ross's hand gripped the steering wheel tensely, and he concentrated completely on the darkened highway in front of him, his jaw set in a hard line.

It was with almost a sense of relief that Melinda realized the car had finally pulled onto the tree-lined street in front of her apartment. Miserably she reached for the door handle. "Thank you very much for dinner. Good night."

"Melinda, wait!"

There was a loud click, and she realized that Ross had automatically locked the passenger door. "Let me out, please," she said, her voice shaking.

"No," came the heavy reply. "I can't let things end like this." He reached over and touched her shoulder gently. "What are we fighting about, anyhow?"

"You tell me." She couldn't bear to meet his eyes.

"Look at me, honey." Ross turned her to face him. "I don't know what happened back in the restaurant, and I don't care. Can't we just forget it, and remember yesterday instead?"

Her gaze locked with his. "What about yesterday?"

His other hand cupped her chin. "You remember what happened," he practically whispered. "I kissed you and almost went up in flames."

Melinda swallowed convulsively. "Don't talk like that."

"I won't talk at all, Melinda," he uttered thickly, "if you'll just let me hold you right now!" Without waiting for an answer, Ross pulled her into his arms and held her tightly against his tense, powerful frame.

This was what she had ached for the entire evening, Melinda realized silently. Being held in his heated embrace had been all she could think about. "Ross," she breathed against the supple leather of his jacket.

His eyes glittered down at her. "I go crazy when you say my name like that!"

Hardly aware of what she was doing, Melinda impulsively brushed a light finger across his lips. "You have a fascinating mouth, did anyone ever tell you that?"

His entire body trembled. "Don't tease me. Not now."

"Who's teasing?" she murmured softly, and touched each corner of his astonished mouth with a feather-light kiss.

"Melinda!" he exclaimed in disbelief.

"What?" She sighed against the taut line of his jaw. Where had she suddenly found the courage to do this? It felt so utterly reckless and wanton, whispering butterfly kisses along his rough skin.

A shiver ran through him with each light kiss. "What are you doing?" Ross groaned. "Trying to seduce me?"

"Don't you like it for a woman to kiss you that way?" Melinda taunted daringly.

"*Like* it? Oh, baby, come here!" Practically driven over the edge, Ross crushed his lips hungrily down on hers. She arched her soft body to his with an eagerness born out of newly discovered love. It was still too soon to tell him of her feelings, but she could show him, in every way imaginable. Melinda wrapped her arms around his neck, savoring every texture of him. His plundering mouth tasted of tobacco and coffee, and his dark hair still bore the fresh balsam scent of his shampoo.

It was Melinda's turn to shiver as Ross's tongue demanded and coaxed a response she was only too willing to give, as it plucked the sweet moistness of her mouth. And then, his lips were everywhere, imprinting his burning brand on her cheeks, her throat, and down along the delicate skin of her collarbone, toward the shadowy cleft between her breasts. All the while, those firm hands molded her more tightly against him, traveling down to the base of her spine, and then, spreading out until they reached her hips.

"Ross!" she exclaimed in shock as his hands now moved upward past her rib cage and closed possessively over each breast.

"Let me touch you, honey," he implored huskily. "Just for a moment!"

Even through the knit material, he could feel her nipples hardening beneath his fingers. Melinda quivered from the exquisite pleasure of this new sensation.

"Does that excite you, Melinda?" His own voice actually shook. "Do you like it when I touch you there?"

"Oh!" She bit back the faint protest.

Ross interpreted this as encouragement, and he began to caress her even more boldly. "You're so soft and sweet, did you know that?" His words were heavy as he pulled aside the sweater fabric from her shoulders, exposing the lacy top of her pink brassiere. It was a wispy French confection of embroidered silk and revealed more than just a glimpse of smooth, creamy flesh.

"No!" Aroused but still embarrassed, Melinda instinctively pushed away his hands.

"What is it?"

Hastily, she drew the dress back over her shoulders and struggled for composure.

Ross drew in his breath. "Am I going too quickly for you, sweetheart?"

Melinda sat up straight and adjusted her clinging clothing. "It's time I was getting back inside," she said in a different tone. "It *is* a school night."

Those dark brown eyes stared at her questioningly. "Have I shocked you?" When Melinda avoided his gaze and stared mutely out of the window, he gave a reluctant sigh. "I'll walk you to your door now."

"Thank you" was the only response she could manage. How could she explain to Ross that it was all happening too fast for her overloaded senses to assimilate at once. And although she did not consider herself to be a prude, the front seat of an automobile was not the place Melinda thought proper for— Oh, why didn't she just come right out and admit it? As much as she wanted this man to hold her and make love to her, she needed to know that it at least meant something special to Ross, as well.

Meanwhile, Ross summoned up every last ounce of self-control and forced himself to get out of the car. Never before in his life had a woman ever aroused him this way. He was actually shaking as he walked around to the passenger side and opened the door for Melinda.

The silvery sliver of a new moon illuminated the concrete walkway to the apartment door. Ross hovered above her in silence as she fumbled for her keys. "I want to thank you for a lovely dinner." Melinda tried to keep her tone casual.

"You're welcome." He stared down at her, an alien glitter in his brown eyes.

He seemed to be waiting for something, but what? she wondered nervously. Melinda pushed the door open, unable to dispel the tension that screamed inside every pore. But Ross remained almost resolutely on the other side of the threshold. It was as if he were aware that this represented an invisible line he dare not cross. Melinda cleared her throat. "Well, it's getting late—" *Oh, Lord, just look at him,* she thought in amazement. How was it possible for a man to be so devastatingly attractive? If she were a more sophisticated woman, she would certainly know how to seduce him. But as it stood at this moment, Melinda felt as inept as a teenager on a first date.

"Yes," he said with a tinge of regret. "It is late."

What was wrong? she wondered, seized with panic. Why wasn't he saying anything else? All of Melinda's feminine assurance seemed to evaporate in an instant. Is this what it felt like to love someone?

"Why are you looking at me like that?" Ross inquired hoarsely.

"Forget it."

"What if I can't forget it?" He stepped into the entryway and towered ominously above her. "A woman looks like that at a man and he just falls apart." His strong arms grasped her waist so tightly Melinda bit her lip.

"What are you saying?"

His mouth was set in a grim line. "Do you really have to ask, Melinda?" When there was no response, he pulled her body roughly against his rigid body, molding her hips with his hands. Those hard, muscled thighs pressed into hers, and it was impossible to conceal his frank, male arousal.

"Oh!" was all she could gasp.

"Does it shock you?" he grated out against her earlobe. "Do you see what you do to me, honey?"

Melinda was unable to suppress a quiver, or the involuntary reaction of her fingers as they dug into the leather jacket. "It doesn't shock me," she murmured, and actually started to melt into the embrace.

His eyes were now wide and astonished. "Melinda!"

It was heavenly to feel him so close. He felt so vital and alive. Ross's powerfully masculine body surged against hers and there was no doubt in her own fevered mind exactly what would happen next. "Are you just going to stand here talking?" she breathed boldly against the sinewy, heated cord of his neck. "Or are you going to kiss me good-night?"

Ross gave an astonished groan. "Are you trying to make me lose my mind?"

"Just . . . just a good-night kiss."

"Melinda . . ." His voice caught in his throat. "What are you telling me?"

It was delicious and mortifying at the same time to confess. "I liked it when we kissed."

"Sweetheart." His gaunt face came alive with awe and wonderment. "Do you *want* me?"

She lowered her eyes self-consciously. "Yes."

But if this admission sent chills down her own spine, it was nothing compared to the effect it had on Ross. "My sweet, beautiful Melinda!" he rasped before claiming her lips with an intense hunger he had never shown before. Now his hands traveled down from her hips to cup her rounded derriere with intimate possession. "I want you so much it's tearing me apart inside!"

Oh, yes, yes! That's the way she felt as well, Melinda agreed silently. To be held in his arms this way—to feel the dizzying touch of his mouth and his hands. But although she prided herself on being an articulate, verbal human being, she was now completely at a loss for words. She could only show this wonderful man how she felt inside. Melinda gave a faint moan as his tongue stabbed through the soft barrier of her lips and plundered the sweet treasure within.

Even as he held her in this erotic, maddening embrace, Ross still had the presence of mind to fling out one arm and slam the front door shut behind them. "We're really alone now," he growled as his teeth bit lightly on the tender flesh of her earlobe. "And there's no one to stop us!" The urgency of his deep voice grew as he pinned her yielding body against the closed door and began to grind his hips into hers in a disturbingly intimate motion.

"Ross!" His raw desire thrilled and frightened her.

"Can you feel just how badly I need you?" he muttered thickly against her tousled hair. "I mean to have you, Melinda!"

His daring words caused a delicious shudder through the entire core of her being. He would take her tonight, Melinda thought wildly, and no power on earth could prevent it from happening. She had waited almost twenty-five years for this night, and now the waiting would soon be over. Ross Kendall would be the man who would make her a woman in every sense of the word. She didn't even protest as his deft fingers began to peel away the angora sweater dress, down past her shoulders, over her trembling arms, and then to her waist. But when he tugged the stretch material further toward her hips, Melinda stiffened for an embarrassed moment.

"Let me, darling," he urged huskily, "let me undress you!" And in another moment, the dress lay on the hardwood floor in a crumpled heap, and those knowing fingers started to unfasten her lacy pink brassiere.

"Don't—" she started to protest in embarrassment, but it was too late. The cool air hit her bare skin.

"You're so beautiful," he said as he feasted his eyes hungrily on her naked breasts.

"Don't look!" Melinda crossed her arms over the bare skin hastily. No man had ever seen her like this.

With infinite gentleness, he pulled away her arms. "How can you be so shy when you're so utterly exquisite?" Almost reverently, he kissed each pink tip, and then his hands closed over each orb possessively. "You're satin and velvet in my fingers."

She almost staggered against him now. If there were secrets of her body to unlock, she wanted Ross to be the one to discover them. She was on fire for him

now, almost mindless with excitement. She barely
noticed that he had removed his jacket and shirt until he had lifted her in his arms, pressing her tightly
against his powerful, hair-roughened chest.

"Show me your bedroom," he whispered roughly
against the pale silk of her hair.

In silence, she gestured toward the back hallway
and then buried her face shyly into his sleek, muscled shoulder. It was going to happen now, she
thought in amazement. In a few moments, there
would be no turning back.

Dimly she was aware of being carried down the
cool, dark corridor and into the dark bedroom. A
faint ray of moonlight streamed in through the window, softly illuminating the eyelet pastel bedspread
and lacy pillows.

"So feminine and sweet," Ross murmured approvingly as he set her down on the full-size bed,
"just like you." And then he pushed Melinda back
against the pillows and kissed her with a strange new
urgency. His lips traveled down the sensitive column
of her throat, burning a trail of liquid fire toward her
breasts. "And you taste like honey," he rasped as his
mouth descended on one perfect pink nub.

"Yes!" Melinda whispered into his dark hair, as
Ross's hungry tongue flicked back and forth over the
sensitized tip. "Touch me there!" She was being
driven over the edge of madness and no longer cared.
She wanted everything this wonderful man could give
her, and she wanted to give everything to him, as well.

Her words seemed to inflame his already-heated
passion. "Yes, darling." A muscle throbbed in his
taut neck. "I'll touch you everywhere!"

His hands began to caress the gentle curve of her thighs, and suddenly he was easing his weight on top of her. When Melinda gave an involuntary tremor, he smiled in dark satisfaction. "That's only the beginning of what I'm going to make you feel!" he uttered against the silken skin of her stomach. "I intend to make you forget every man you've ever known before tonight is through!" Ross paused significantly. "When I've finished making love to you, Peter Harrison won't even be a memory!" His fingers slid along the delicate lace waistband of her bikini panties.

A thought occurred to her dimly. What was he saying? Did he actually think that she and Peter had been lovers? The very idea tainted the beauty of what was about to happen, and Melinda knew she had to tell Ross, explain somehow. "You're wrong," she whispered in protest, "so very wrong!"

"Wrong about what?" he breathed thickly.

"Peter Harrison and I...we were never lovers." She stared up into his dark, surprised eyes. "In fact, the truth is—"

Something dangerous flickered in his expression. "The truth is what? What is it you have to tell me?"

"There's never been anyone. *Ever.*"

She could feel his powerful body actually shudder. "What do you mean...there's never been anyone?"

Melinda felt a heated flush of embarrassment. "I've never let anyone else ever touch me like this, before you."

The reality behind her words finally struck him, and Ross turned white as a sheet. "Are you trying to tell me...?" His jaw clenched.

His body became taut above hers, and Melinda gazed up at him in confusion. "What's the matter?"

He practically choked. "How can you even ask me that?"

"I don't understand—"

His face remained ashen. "You and Peter Harrison... I was so sure that the two of you—"

"Well, you were wrong."

"Why *me?*" Ross demanded now. "You've never let another man touch you. Why, all of a sudden, do you let *me?*"

Because I'm in love with you, Ross Kendall! she wanted to cry out. But every fiber of her being protested against such a confession. Melinda had never felt so painfully vulnerable. Instead, she forced a vague smile and shrugged. "Honestly, what are you making such a fuss about, Ross?"

He sat bolt upright. "A fuss? Is that what you call it? A *fuss?*"

Melinda gave a bright, artificial little laugh. "A girl has to learn sometime, after all."

Ross's eyes darkened. "Is that what this is all about? You need some lessons in lovemaking so you've come to me?"

Suddenly self-conscious, she drew the quilt over her seminude body. "That isn't it at all!"

Ross gave a hollow laugh. "I should have known. I was an idiot to think there was any other reason. *Now* it all makes sense."

"What on earth are you talking about?"

He rose up from the bed. The taut muscles of his bare chest actually glistened with sweat. "It isn't necessary to put on the act anymore, Melinda." The words were scathing.

She flung the blanket away angrily. "What act?"

His nostrils flared. "The act you're putting on this very minute. Trying to tempt me... distract me with your exquisite body." He forced himself to turn away from the sight of her. "It almost worked, too." The words came out like chipped ice. "You almost acquired the experience you seemed to need so badly."

Melinda reached for the pastel silk robe she always kept by the bed. She covered herself quickly, then tightened the sash with a furious tug. "You actually believe I let you make love to me because I needed *experience*?"

"Correction, we *almost* made love. You have no idea how lucky you were. A few moments more and—"

"How dare you!" Her eyes blazed. "What kind of woman do you think I am, Ross Kendall?"

He raked a hand through his matted hair and once again his entire body shook. "I'll tell you exactly the kind of woman you are, Melinda Clarke. Innocent, proper and prim, but oh, so very logical. You decided it was time to learn about sex and chose me to be your teacher. I suppose I ought to be flattered."

She couldn't believe what she was hearing. How could the man possibly think such a sordid thing? She drew in her breath. "Let me get this straight. You think I wanted to—be with you because of..."

"Curiosity," he finished frostily.

"Of all the nerve!" Melinda hurled a pillow at his stomach. "That's what you believe? That I was *curious?*"

He caught the next few pillows deftly in one hand and tossed each one back onto the bed. "You're beautiful and bright. You could have any man you want."

"So you keep telling me," she shot back acidly.

Hard hands descended onto her shoulders, burning through the thin silk of the robe. "Give me one other sane reason. Another reason that could possibly make sense!" he ground out.

Melinda struggled to free herself from his angry grip, but Ross held fast. "Let me go."

"No," he uttered thickly. "I almost took you just now, Melinda. You were going to let me be your very first man." The thought seemed to torment him. "The very first," he whispered against her hair.

The first and only, she wanted to cry out, but the words just died in Melinda's throat. Frustrated, she tried to pull away, but instead, the action caused Ross to lose his balance and they both tumbled back onto the mattress. "Oh!"

The fall left Ross sprawled on top of her, the folds of the silk robe partially open to reveal tantalizing glimpses of her body.

"This is madness!" he groaned. "I can't stand much more of this!" For one long, tortured moment he buried his lips in the soft hollow between her breasts and ground his hips against hers. Then, with a convulsive shudder, he forced himself up from the bed. "I should keep you down on that mattress and make love until you scream for mercy." His eyes were dark and inflamed. "I should take you and say to hell with the consequences!"

Melinda was so hurt and confused that she was beyond caring. "Consequences?" she gave a bitter laugh. "You needn't worry about that, Mr. Kendall. Please rest assured I wasn't attempting to trap you in any way."

Something odd flickered in his eyes. "You've got it all wrong, honey. If anyone would have been trapped, it would have been *you.*"

"And what does that mean?"

There was a strange determination in the hard set of Ross's jaw. "You're an old-fashioned girl, Melinda."

She frowned. "Hardly."

He ignored her. "But then, the truth of the matter is, I'm an old-fashioned man." Ross took one last hungry glance at Melinda and, without another word, stalked out of the bedroom. Seconds later, the door slammed, and not long afterward, there was the sound of his Jaguar screeching off into the moonlit night.

Melinda trembled in the chill of the darkened room. What had happened? What had gone wrong? The answer was painfully obvious. Ross Kendall didn't want anything to do with virgins. It was her own fault, of course. Trying to maintain the charade of being so proper and prim all these years. And just look where it had gotten her! The man she loved now considered her to be a stiff, virginal Miss Goodie Two Shoes. She was old-fashioned, straitlaced Melinda Clarke, all right. It was an image she had struggled to achieve in order to live down her past. Suddenly, after eight long years, she wondered why it had been so important to suppress such a vital part of herself.

Now, in the midst of her pain over Ross, it occurred to Melinda that the past eight years may have been peaceful and serene, but they had not been particularly happy. On the other hand, despite the notoriety of being Little Lindy, her youth had been a time of joyful exuberance.

Melinda stared at her tear-streaked face in the mirror. How very strange. Until this moment, she hadn't even been aware that she was crying.

Chapter Nine

Somehow Melinda managed to make it through the next morning. During the break between classes, she sat listlessly in her office, overwhelmed by the strangest sensation of melancholy. It was impossible to force the memory of last night from her mind. Melinda could still feel the burning imprint of Ross's lips on her skin. She had to suppress a shiver as she remembered the feel of his hard, athletic body against hers. There was no denying that he had wanted her every bit as badly as she had wanted him. In the cool shadows of her bedroom, Melinda had let down all physical barriers for the first time in her life. But what had it all meant? she thought bitterly. Ross had suddenly rejected her. The entire experience had been utterly humiliating.

Nervously Melinda tapped her slender fingers on the desktop and noticed the corner of an envelope sticking out from beneath the green felt blotter. With a faint sigh, she recalled having placed the legal-sized envelope in that place months ago, in fact, on the day she had taken up her teaching post at Perryville. Inside were several photos of her family that Melinda had originally intended to frame and hang on her office wall. That is, until she met her office-mate, Selene, and decided she didn't want to share such personal mementos after all.

Now Melinda gazed fondly at the pictures. There were several of her brothers and an old snapshot of her mother dressed in jungle fatigues with a camera slung around her neck, but the last photograph was Melinda's favorite by far. Two years ago, at Christmastime, the entire Clarke family had posed in front of the house. How she missed that wonderful creepy old Gothic home she had grown up in. Her brothers spent endless gleeful hours trying to convince her that the place was haunted. She giggled at the memory. But to their dismay, Melinda had turned the tables on their silly boyish pranks. Even at the mere age of seven, she had been a prodigy jokester, more than a match for three mischievous teenagers. All it had taken to frighten the wits out of Gary, Dev and Wyler had been a couple of old puppets, a long silk scarf and a can of fluorescent spray paint. The midnight monster she created from these simple materials would later be chronicled in a classic "Life With Lindy" Halloween strip. Despite herself, Melinda smiled. What fun life had been back then. How utterly carefree. Little Lindy had never been afraid of anything, or intimidated by anyone. She was engulfed by a wave of nostalgia for that happier time.

Just then, the office door burst open and shattered her reverie. "Good morning, Selene."

"Good morning," came the curt greeting. Since their quarrel on Monday, a kind of awkward truce existed between the two of them. A truce born of necessity. They might dislike each other intensely, but from a practical point of view, they still had to share an office.

Melinda placed the photos facedown on the desk and examined her watch. It was almost time for her freshman composition class. She stood up and reached for the lesson plan. "It's all yours."

Selene looked disparagingly around the tiny room. "Oh, gee, thanks," she muttered. Then she watched in silence as Melinda walked out the door. After waiting a moment, Selene glanced over curiously at the pile of photographs on Melinda's desk. The chubby brunette hesitated for just a moment and then strolled over to the desk.

Normally Melinda spent her lunch hour in the pleasant atmosphere of the teachers' lounge. Today, however, she needed to get away for a while and clear the troubled thoughts from her mind. At noon, she drove off campus into downtown Perryville. After treating herself to a delightfully greasy cheeseburger and chocolate milk shake at the local fast-food restaurant, she took a leisurely stroll down Main Street. This was a charming, tree-lined avenue with numerous Victorian-style buildings along a stretch of old cobblestone. Just as Melinda was getting back into her car, she heard a familiar voice behind her.

"I've been looking for you," Ross Kendall said quietly.

Her heart lurched. "Really?" she responded in a shaky tone. Was it Melinda's imagination, or did the man actually have dark circles under his eyes?

"Where can we talk?" he muttered uneasily and raked a hand through his hair.

"Oh, do we have anything to talk about?"

"You're damn right we do."

Trying to hide her nervousness, Melinda affected a casual air and leaned against the hood of the Mustang. "I thought we discussed everything last night."

"No."

"I see," she retorted crisply. "And exactly what *else* did you wish to add to your numerous sensitive and flattering remarks from last night? So far, you've defined me as prim, naive, old-fashioned and motivated by an almost pitiful curiosity."

A muscle in his jaw tensed. "I never meant that at all." He gripped her shoulders. "I'm trying to explain, if you'd just let me!" His hard fingers bit into the thin material of her linen jacket, and Melinda flinched involuntarily. "Oh, God, I'm sorry!" He released his grip hastily and stared down at the pavement with unseeing eyes. "How did you sleep last night, Melinda?" came the strained inquiry. "Did you have sweet, pleasant dreams?"

She quirked an eyebrow. "I beg your pardon?"

Ross twisted his mouth. "I spent a sleepless, miserable night."

"I'm delighted to hear it." She crossed her arms. Melinda was not in a forgiving mood. All she could think of was the pain and humiliation this man had caused her.

He looked up with an odd expression on his gaunt face. "That's an odd reaction. Here I thought you were such a compassionate young soul."

Melinda glanced at her watch with mock impatience. "Is this going to take very long? I happen to be on my lunch hour."

"Would you listen to me, for the love of heaven? I'm trying to apologize!" Ross cupped her chin in his hand with incredible gentleness. "Don't you know how much it wrenched my gut walking out on you like that?" His words came out as a harsh, shocking whisper against her ear. "I pushed you away and said angry, bitter things I didn't mean. Don't you have any idea just how badly I wanted to stay? I haven't been able to think of anything else since that night on my terrace."

Melinda quivered. "Please, I don't want to talk about this!" How could she make him understand? It was too painful. The wounds were still fresh.

He touched her cheek sadly. "You still don't get it, do you? If I had taken your innocence last night, you would have ended up hating me."

"You're wrong," she said, her voice trembling.

"Am I?" Ross's tone was hollow, defeated. "I don't think so."

It was such sweet torture to feel him this close again, his thighs barely brushing against hers. "I could never hate you." Melinda stared at him helplessly. "Never."

A shudder ran through his powerful frame. "Melinda!" For a moment the two of them seemed unaware that this was a public parking area, and several passersby were glancing curiously in their direction.

Ross pulled her roughly into his arms. "Is this what you want?"

It must show through every pore of her being, she thought with a shiver. All he had to do was touch her this way. "Don't tease me." Melinda's eyes welled with tears.

"Who's teasing?" he uttered hoarsely, his lips scant inches from her own. "All I want to do right now is kiss the breath out of you!" Ross's broad hands caressed her back and he lowered his mouth toward hers.

But at the very instant of the electric contact, the jarring blast of a car horn shattered the moment. Ross pulled away as if he had been stung. "What the hell am I doing?" he exclaimed thickly. "I must be out of my mind!"

"Well, fine!" Melinda accused in a hurt voice. "How very fortunate that you managed to come to your senses just in the nick of time." Still shaking, she lunged for the door handle.

"What are you doing?" came the harsh inquiry.

"What does it look like?" she snapped. "I'm leaving!"

"Wait!"

There was a strange vulnerability to his plea. "What for?" Melinda responded fully, and slid into the driver's seat.

"We have to talk about this." He reached through the open window and swiftly removed the key from the ignition.

"Of all the—"

"No, just listen," Ross said grimly. "I can't let you leave until I explain."

"I'm waiting," she said through tight lips.

His dark eyes narrowed. "We almost made love last night."

"I don't want to hear this!"

A vein in his temple throbbed. "Well, you're going to hear it, anyway. It would have been wrong, I realize that so clearly now." He hesitated solemnly. "You're a virgin, for heaven's sake."

"Thank you so much for reminding me." Melinda stared down at the steering wheel.

"You should wait to give yourself to the man you love. The man you're going to marry! I'm not going to ruin it for you, honey." Ross smashed his fist into the roof of the car. "You'll still be pure on your wedding night with Harrison."

Her jaw practically dropped. "What are you talking about?"

There was sad irony in his eyes. "Haven't you heard yet? Peter Harrison told me about his honorable intentions."

"What?"

"He was set to propose before that trip to Venezuela."

Melinda swallowed uncomfortably. "This is all news to me."

"Why so surprised?" he said mockingly. "Surely you expected him to propose one of these days. After all, the two of you make a perfect couple."

She flinched as if he'd struck her. "How can you say that?" Her voice almost cracked.

His knuckles showed white. "It's true, isn't it? The beautiful princess always marries the handsome prince. That's what it says in all the fairy tales."

"This is real life."

"And what would you know about real life in that remote ivory tower of yours?" came the scathing retort.

"Ivory tower?" she sputtered. "In case you've forgotten, I happen to be Little Lindy."

"No, that was long ago, in another fairy tale." Ross shrugged cynically. "That person is just another myth now. You told me yourself that she no longer exists. Why, nowadays, you're just as straight and proper as they come. I'll bet you've never even gotten a parking ticket."

There was an awkward pause. "You don't know anything."

"I know everything, that's my problem." He gave a regretful sigh and tossed the keys into her lap. "You'd best be getting back to school. I'm sure you're never late for classes, either."

With a shaking hand, she thrust the key into the ignition. "I've heard just about enough!"

"You're angry now," Ross uttered hoarsely, "but that's just wounded pride, nothing more. Later on, you'll thank me."

"I highly doubt that." She bit the words back.

"I'd rather cut off my right arm than hurt you, Melinda. Don't you know that by now?"

She stared at him in disbelief as he turned and walked toward the other side of the parking lot, a defeated slope to his broad shoulders. A moment later, he gunned the engine of the Jaguar and peeled off into the busy street.

Melinda sank back against her seat in utter frustration. How was such a thing possible? Could a man of Ross Kendall's intelligence really be so incredibly obtuse? By what bizarre equation had he arrived at such an unbelievable conclusion? Did he actually think that a man like Peter Harrison was her idea of a Prince Charming? Was Ross so blind that he could not see how she was almost dying for love of him?

For the rest of the afternoon, she was haunted by thoughts of that disturbing confrontation. When she was back in her office at the end of the day, even the strange looks and cryptic comments of Selene Monroe were unable to penetrate her awareness. She could only replay Ross's scathing words over and over again in her mind. The man considered her to be Miss Goodie Two Shoes in the extreme. All right, it was true—she had never received a traffic ticket in her life, and her conduct had been beyond reproach during her entire adulthood. Did that make her the perfect mate for Peter Harrison? A man without an ounce of whimsy or mischief in his soul?

"See you tomorrow, Miss Clarke," called out Brenda Matthews, who was lounging comfortably beneath the shade of one of the magnificent old oak trees.

"Good night, Brenda." Melinda smiled back in faint amusement as the teenager attempted to conceal the huge heart she had scribbled on the cover of her notebook. Even upside down, Melinda's sharp eyesight could discern the heavily emblazoned initials—B.M. & P.H. Perhaps it was simply a coincidence, but on the other hand... She squinted in the bright afternoon sunlight. Did everyone in Perryville believe that Peter Harrison was the perfect Prince Charming except herself?

Melinda hesitated and glanced around critically. In the warm glow of early May, the turn-of-the-century brick building laced with a mantle of ivy reminded her of something else Ross had said. *She lived in an ivory tower,* he had told her. Was that the truth? she wondered now. Was that the kind of life she led at the Perryville Academy?

Could he possibly be right? Melinda tried to think of a single time in the past eight years when she had disobeyed a single rule or flouted authority with even the most minor infraction. And when had she played even the most simple prank during all those years? *Never,* that was when.

And here was the wonderful result. The man she loved considered her to be as fragile as a piece of porcelain. Delicate, naive and unapproachable. The perfect match for a stiff-necked bore like Peter Harrison.

Melinda gave a bitter laugh. Perhaps it was time to start being true to herself again. She'd show Mr. Ross Kendall just how seriously he had misjudged her. There was still a Little Lindy inside of the prissy Miss Clarke. She'd teach him a lesson he'd never forget.

Little Lindy was back!

Chapter Ten

As any faithful reader of the comic strip will tell you, the outrageous pranks of Little Lindy were seldom deterred by guard dogs, car alarms or computerized home security systems. Not when you had a scientific genius for a father and a daredevil journalist for a mother.

At precisely eight o'clock the next morning, Ross Kendall stalked out of his rambling white colonial mansion with a scowl on his rugged face. It had been another sleepless night haunted by visions of Melinda. He slammed the front door grimly. What kind of fool was he being to turn down what she had offered him so freely? The hurt expression in those exquisite blue eyes yesterday had made matters even worse. Each time he walked away from her it was an agony. Why was he putting himself through such torture? What did he care *why* Melinda wanted him to make love to her? Wasn't it heaven enough that this beautiful, sweet creature had trembled in his arms and let her soft body yield so willingly against his? What more could any man ask?

Ross groaned painfully. The truth had shocked him down to the very core of his being. The night he had walked out of Melinda's bedroom, he had taken a good look at the man he had become in the past seven years, and he hated what he had seen.

All during his ruthless pursuit of Melinda Clarke, he had been convinced that his feelings for her were simple desire. But that night had come the aching realization that his true feelings ran far deeper. He needed Melinda in his life permanently. He wanted her to love him. But now he knew with an aching sadness that this would never happen.

Wearily he reached for his car keys. It was better this way, he thought with glum assurance. It was best for his own sanity to break it off now, before the situation got out of hand. It would have been far more unbearable to make love to Melinda only to lose her to Peter Harrison, anyway. In his heart, Ross knew that she would eventually marry the handsome young attorney to whom she was far better suited.

Every step down the stone stairway jolted his tense body. Suddenly a sight in the drive below stopped Ross dead in his tracks. "What the—" It was a sight so startling that his jaw actually dropped, and his expensive leather briefcase went smashing to the ground. In utter astonishment, Ross stumbled along the gravel toward the green Jaguar and just continued to stare. It was no longer *green*. The elegant

British automobile gleamed in the morning sunlight, now a bright, shocking pink.

"Daddy!" a voice exclaimed behind him. "What happened to your car?"

Ross looked like a man who had just been flattened by a tornado. "It's pink!"

"It looks so cool!" Jenny threw down her schoolbooks and ran over to inspect the Jaguar more closely.

"Cool?" Ross's voice cracked. "You think it looks *cool?"*

The little girl nodded enthusiastically. "Pink is the 'in' color."

"Uh-huh."

"It's like a giant stick of bubble gum!"

"Oh, great!" he groaned.

She turned her admiring eyes from the shiny automobile. "When did you decide to paint it, Daddy?"

There was a strange expression on his sun-bronzed face. "I didn't."

"If you didn't, then who did?"

"Someone is obviously playing a prank, a very expensive prank—" Ross stopped in midsentence.

"You mean it's a joke?" Jenny giggled. "Who would want to play a joke on you?"

For just a moment, a light flickered in his dark eyes. Then, slowly, disbelievingly, he murmured, "I think I have a pretty good idea."

Melinda stifled another yawn as she walked up the main staircase to her first class. It had been a rather long night, but as far as she was concerned, the results were well worth the effort. Spray-painting Ross

Kendall's car was reckless and irresponsible, but Melinda was sincerely convinced that such a radical gesture was the only way to prove to the man how utterly wrong he had been about her. Old-fashioned, straitlaced princesses who lived in ivory towers did not go around painting expensive foreign cars pink in the middle of the night.

"Hello...Melinda." Otis Wilkins greeted her at the top of the stairs with a broad grin, followed by a wink.

"Good morning, Otis." She glanced at him curiously.

"I never would have guessed," he blurted out. "Not in a million years!"

"Guessed what?" She was suddenly apprehensive.

"Personally I think it's terrific!" interrupted a petite figure in a gray Perryville sweatshirt and pants.

"I beg your pardon?" Melinda turned her attention to Penelope Rourke.

The physical education instructor gave a good-natured chuckle. "Let me tell you, Melinda. This is really going to put our school on the map!" Without another word, she smiled at Otis, and the two of them walked down the hall.

Bewildered, Melinda proceeded toward her office. At this early hour, only a few students were visible in the corridors. All of them seemed to be staring at her oddly and whispering to one another.

Mystified, she arrived at her office, only to find the door unlocked and Selene Monroe already sitting at her desk. It was almost as if the dark-haired teacher had been waiting for her arrival. "Good morning, Melinda," she said, practically sneering.

"Hello, Selene." Melinda sensed something different in the air.

The other woman fidgeted with a silver letter opener. "Or would you prefer me to call you *Lindy?*"

"Excuse me?" Her voice shook.

"That was pretty careless of you." Selene gave a hard smile. "Leaving all those old photographs on your desk. It was almost an invitation. Didn't you think I'd be just a little bit curious?"

Melinda quirked an eyebrow. Damn, the family pictures! She'd been so wrapped up in her problems with Ross Kendall, it had completely escaped her mind. "You went through my personal possessions?"

Selene shrugged. "The window was open, and there was a sudden breeze. What can I say? Those pictures simply blew off your desktop. I was just doing you a favor by picking them up off the floor."

"I'm *sure.*"

"Imagine my amazement to discover the striking resemblance between your mother and the famous Joanna Prescott." Selene's tone turned spiteful. "Just out of curiosity, I happened to be glancing through the personnel records, and what a coincidence! Joanna Prescott is your mother's name."

Melinda drew a breath. "That's none of your business."

"No? That's not what the board of trustees thinks."

She felt sick. "The board of trustees?"

"Well, I felt it was my duty to inform them." Selene gave a nasty laugh. "It doesn't take a nuclear scientist to arrive at the conclusion that the high-and-mighty Miss Melinda Clarke is actually the world-renowned precocious brat known as Little Lindy." There was a triumphant pause. "They'll be calling a special meeting some time next week to discuss how badly it might reflect on the school."

"I don't believe you." Melinda ran an angry hand over her braid. "That's outrageous!"

"Believe whatever you want." Her office-mate pursed her thin lips. "I happen to have an aunt on the board, and it's a rather conservative group. A member of the faculty at Perryville is supposed to set a proper example for the students. One's personal history should be above reproach." There was another pause. "Don't take my word for it. Just examine your employment contract."

Stunned, Melinda gazed down at her colleague. "Why would you do something like this, Selene?" she asked quietly. "Do you dislike me so much?"

The other woman shrugged. "I waited three years for Peter to finally ask me out, and just a week after our first date, *you* had to come to town."

"Listen to me, Selene. I'm not interested in Peter Harrison!"

"I really don't care how *you* feel." Selene rose from her chair. "All that matters is how Peter feels. When he finds out about your lurid little past, he'll drop you like a hot potato! A junior partner at Caton and Henderson can't afford to be encumbered with the scandalous former Little Lindy."

Melinda gave a heavy sigh and reached for the day's lesson plans. "As far as I'm concerned, Selene, you're welcome to have Peter. I could care less."

Throughout the morning, it became quite obvious that Selene Monroe had taken great pleasure in revealing Melinda's secret to the entire school. There wasn't a single student in the Perryville Academy who wasn't now aware that the infamous Little Lindy was the school's own Miss Clarke. In every class, her students giggled and whispered amongst one another. At one point, Lonnie Ellison grinned at her in the hallway and murmured. "I think it's so neat!"

But Brenda Matthews waited until her favorite teacher disappeared down the corridor and turned thoughtfully to her best friend. "Yeah, I think she's the totally coolest teacher we ever had, but I hear she's getting fired!"

"Oh, c'mon!"

"Hey, you know what?" Brenda mused through her chewing gum. "If we got all our parents to sign a petition, maybe they couldn't get rid of Miss Clarke, after all."

"I only wish," Lonnie said with a sigh. "But you know how uptight that board of trustees is."

Neither of them noticed the distressed expression on the face of the little girl who stood behind them. "They want to fire Miss Clarke?" she exclaimed in a cultured British accent.

"Yeah, kid." Brenda nodded. "That's why you, me, Lonnie and everybody else has to do something to stop them."

* * *

The idea of spending her lunch hour as the center of attention in the teachers' lounge was unbearable to Melinda. With Selene inexplicably out of the office, she settled down at her own desk to gather her thoughts. Then, as if the previous events of the morning hadn't been odd enough, Melinda received an unexpected long-distance call from Peter Harrison.

"Hi, Peter," she said, attempting to sound enthusiastic. "How are you?"

"Why didn't you tell me before?" were practically the first words out of his mouth.

"Tell you about what?"

"About being Little Lindy."

Melinda gave a weary sigh. "Good news travels fast."

"It's not a joke! Mr. Caton, himself, called me. Do you have any idea what an awkward position this puts me in?"

"I beg your pardon?"

Uncomfortably, Peter cleared his throat. "Caton and Henderson is a very conservative low-profile firm, Melinda. The woman I marry has to be above reproach."

"Marry? What are you talking about?" She practically sputtered.

"Please, Melinda," the voice on the other end of the wire urged. "Don't make this more difficult than it already is. I can't see you anymore."

"Fine with me!"

Indignant and relieved, Melinda slammed down the receiver.

Suddenly in need of air, Melinda escaped to the parking area to drive off-campus again. It was a warm day, and she was at least grateful to have chosen to wear a slim cotton knit dress in navy blue with a wide matching belt. It kept her comfortably cool, but just on the outside. On the inside, Melinda felt flushed and nervous. In another week, she would very likely be out of a job. But this was minor compared to the pangs of regret she was now experiencing over Ross Kendall. In the sensible light of day, she wondered if she had been out of her mind last night. What had possessed her to perform such an immature, idiotic prank? It would probably take her entire bank account to have the man's automobile repainted. Surely he had seen his car by now. It was only a matter of time before he would confront her with those angry brown eyes of his. Well, Melinda sighed, maybe she could blame it on a temporary lapse of sanity.

At that moment, something bright pink screeched into the parking lot. "Oh, terrific," she muttered aloud.

Ross slammed the door behind him and stood there tall and ominous. "What do you have to say for yourself, Lindy Clarke?" He folded his arms against his powerful chest.

Nervously she began, "Listen, I can explain."

His mouth tightened. "Just get in," he said as he gestured solemnly toward the passenger side.

"Ross, about your car—"

"Yes, what about it?"

"You have every right to be mad."

"Fine," he retorted grimly. "Now get in the car."

With a sense of apprehension, Melinda walked over to the passenger door and slid inside. A second later, Ross eased his lanky frame back behind the steering wheel and slammed the door shut. There was a long silence, and then, staring straight ahead, he finally gave a deep sigh. "First, I want you to know that I just received a hysterical phone call from my daughter."

Melinda glanced at him in concern. "Jenny? Is she all right?"

"Just fine," came the smooth reply. "Apparently she's more worried about *you.*"

"Oh."

Ross turned to face her. "Jenny begged me to do everything in my power to make sure you don't lose your job at Perryville."

Melinda lowered her eyes. "That isn't necessary."

"No?" He twisted his lips. "Why would you say that? Don't you want to keep your teaching position, Melinda? Or is it that you don't want any favors from me, in particular?"

"It doesn't matter now."

"Oh, it matters," he uttered darkly, "believe me, it matters." Ross cleared his throat. "In any case, it's all been resolved."

She looked at him in puzzlement. "What do you mean?"

He shrugged. "The board of trustees is still reeling from all the angry phone calls received this morning. Evidently, dozens of parents informed the board that they fully intended to withdraw their children from the academy if such a gifted, inspirational teacher like Melinda Clarke was fired."

"Oh?"

"But it wasn't really necessary. You see, not everyone on the board is as hard nosed and reactionary as you might believe."

She was bewildered. "But Selene said—"

His mouth tightened. "Forget Selene Monroe. At this very moment, she's being urged to consider other means of employment."

"She's getting fired?"

"Not exactly, but it's been clear to the board for quite some time that a person of Ms. Monroe's temperament doesn't belong teaching young children." Ross paused significantly. "But we were talking about you, Melinda Prescott Clarke. It turns out that the chairman of the board of trustees, himself, has been a 'Little Lindy' fan for years."

She smiled despite herself. "Really?"

"Really." There was a brief silence. "Besides, I've just finished making my position clear to the chairman of the board of trustees. If they terminate your contract, then they can also forget about the new gymnasium the Kendall family had intended to endow."

"Why would you do that?" Melinda asked softly. "After I ruined your car?"

There was an unexpected glimmer in his eyes. "I wouldn't exactly call it 'ruined.' I might, however, argue with the choice of color."

"Look, if you intend to sue me for damages, I fully intend to reimburse you for the cost of a new paint job."

"Sue you?" He came closer. "Why on earth would I want to sue you? That happens to be one of the most professional paint jobs I've ever seen."

"What are you saying? You don't mind driving around in a hot pink Jaguar?"

"Actually I hate it." He hesitated. "But that's not the point." There was an expression of wonderment on his gaunt face. "I'm just flattered that you cared enough to take all that trouble. I'll bet you were up the entire night working in my driveway." There was another silence. "Would you like to tell me *why?*"

Melinda swallowed. "I'm not the prim, old-fashioned person you seem to think I am. It seemed like the only way to convince you."

Ross drew in his breath. "If I didn't know any better, I'd swear what you did was almost a labor of love."

A tingling sensation shot down through her toes. "Would you?" Her voice was barely audible.

He stared back. "But I know better, don't I, Melinda?"

She gazed blindly out of the window. "Whatever you say."

"Don't you understand, honey?" he uttered roughly. "I've played this down and dirty from the start. Who do you think arranged to send Harrison to the Caribbean?"

"You—you were just helping him out because he's a good lawyer," Melinda stammered.

"I couldn't care less about helping that fool," Ross grumbled. "I just wanted him out of the way, that's all!"

It was suddenly very hot inside the car. "Why?" she whispered.

"You know damn well why!" came the husky reply.

"Tell me." Her blue eyes locked with his, and Melinda felt a delicious shiver of anticipation.

"Because I wanted my chance with you!" he blurted out hastily.

"So you had your chance, and what did you do with it, Mr. Ross Kendall?" Melinda glared at him accusingly. "Absolutely nothing!"

In an angry gesture, he pulled her into his arms. "Nothing? Do you call this nothing?" With a groan, Ross's mouth descended on hers, pressing apart her soft lips with his demanding tongue. Meanwhile, his weight pushed her back against the leather seat. "Is this nothing?" he muttered in heated passion against her eyelids, her cheeks and the rounded smoothness of her throat. He owned her with that wonderful hard mouth.

"Ross, darling!" The endearment escaped her trembling lips before she could stop herself.

"What did you call me?" he breathed harshly.

"Since when do you care?" she tossed back glibly to hide her embarrassment.

"Oh, I care." His jaw tensed, and it made the scars on the rugged line of his face even more vivid. "I've always cared." There was a weary sadness in his tone. "Is that what you want to hear? Does it amuse you to hear me make a fool of myself?"

Something bright and wonderful hovered in the air. "What are you trying to say to me?" Melinda felt the warm glow begin to spread through her heart. "Tell me."

He seemed so oddly vulnerable at that moment. "Don't play with me, Melinda. Can't you see it can never be any good between us? I thought it would be enough just to take you and have you," Ross grated out painfully. "I can't, baby. You're ripping me apart inside, but I can't. It means too much to be just sex."

The confession had humbled him. He sat next to her a raw, exposed nerve, and Melinda wanted to cry out in utter joy. Instead, she took his rough face between her two slender hands. "Don't you understand?" Her eyes brimmed bright with tears. "I feel the same way."

A shudder wracked his powerful body. "You can't!"

"Why can't I?" she protested gently. "You're a wonderful man and I adore you, Ross Kendall." Strange, how easily the words came to her lips now.

"Melinda!" His voice cracked. "Don't tease me!"

She shook her head solemnly. "I've waited almost twenty-five years for a man like you," she continued with blunt honesty. "Why else would I let you make love to me?"

"Oh, God!" He gripped her shoulders tightly. "Tell me, honey. Let me know I'm not dreaming. Let me hear the words!"

Her mouth quivered. "I love you."

"You love me?" Ross shook his head in wonderment. "You *love* me? Oh, baby, don't let me wake up!" With incredible tenderness, he pulled her across his knees so that she half sat, half lay, in his lap. With his firm hands smoothing her back, he lowered his hungry mouth to hers once more. He kissed her with long, drugging kisses that left Melinda gasping for breath. She arched herself up against his tense body and wrapped her arms eagerly around his neck. After several moments, Ross pulled away reluctantly. He stared down at her with an alien glitter in his eyes. "We'd better stop before I take you right here in the parking lot!" His breathing was ragged and unsteady.

Daringly she murmured against his ear, "Why doesn't the teacher just keep you after school?"

A tremor rocked his massive frame. "Keep talking that way and I won't be answerable for my actions, honey!" With a groan, he caressed her sweet, yielding body for a maddening instant, and then, with iron self-control, Ross put her from him resolutely. "Tonight," he promised thickly, "tonight you'd better just watch out, honey. I intend to make love to you until you scream for mercy."

A thrill ran through Melinda. "Ross!"

"But first," he said, "we have to take care of some unfinished business."

"I don't understand."

He shook his head in amazement. "You really don't, do you?" Ross leaned over and pulled a box out of the glove compartment. "I bought this for you this morning when I realized who had spray-painted my car." He pressed his lips together. "You see, that was the first inkling I had that you might feel even the slightest something for me. I was as excited as a teenager."

Melinda glanced at the box curiously. "What is it?" It was a small square covered in dark green velvet.

"Don't you know?" He opened the box and removed a diamond solitaire. "It's an engagement ring."

"Are you asking me to marry you?" She practically gasped.

"No." He looked at her and sighed. "I'm *begging* you to marry me, Melinda."

"Why?" She needed to hear the words.

"Why?" he almost thundered. "How can you even ask that?"

"The words," she whispered softly.

He stared at her tenderly. "Is that what you're waiting to hear, sweetheart? That I love you?" When Melinda nodded mutely, Ross gave a low laugh. "You're more blind than I am, honey. I've loved you since that night on the terrace, but I never thought you could feel the same way about a man who looked like me."

She melted into his arms again. "I think you're the most incredibly attractive man I've ever met." Melinda's lips traveled down the scarred line of his rough cheek with infinite gentleness. "I love everything about you, including your daughter."

His arms tightened possessively. "Oh, God! Is it possible to ever be happier than I am at this very moment?"

Melinda sighed against the fine wool of his suit vest. "Do you think Jenny will mind?"

He gave a chuckle. "Are you kidding? She'll be thrilled!"

"Are you sure?" She was slightly apprehensive. "I've never been a stepmother before."

Ross smoothed the hair back from her forehead affectionately. "I'll let you in on a little secret, honey. Jenny's been hinting all week how much she'd love for the two of us to get married." A shadow flickered briefly across his face. "You see, Jenny's mother never had much time for her, especially later on. She put her in a boarding school so the child wouldn't be in the way of..." He paused. "Her active social life."

Melinda felt a pang of jealousy. "Does it still hurt to think about your wife?" She had to know.

He stared at her in utter disbelief. "Deirdre? She never loved me, and to be truthful, I never loved her, either." Ross cupped her chin in his hands. "I never loved anyone until I met you, Melinda. I swear it. And when you look at me with those beautiful blue eyes of yours, I can only laugh at the pain I felt all those years ago." He shook his head and marveled. "You'll bring me so much joy, sweetheart."

If there was ever a single moment of supreme happiness, Melinda would always look back on this one, as she and Ross clung to each other in that exquisite instant of delicious discovery. And as his kisses became even more passionate and his hands caressed her more and more boldly, she stared up at him. "Ross," Melinda breathed softly.

"What is it, baby?" he murmured hotly against the tender flesh of her earlobe.

"I don't think I can hold out until after school," came the tremulous whisper.

Ross swallowed convulsively. "What?"

She ran a deliberate finger along the line of his angular jaw. "Why don't you take me home right now?"

He shivered. "Are you saying you want to play hooky, Miss Clarke?"

"Mmm-hmm." Melinda leaned forward and loosened his patterned silk tie. "Eight years is far too long to have a perfect attendance record." She daringly unbuttoned the top few buttons of his cotton dress shirt and buried her cheek against the masculine warmth of his hair-roughened chest.

Ross's breathing grew rapid and heavy. "Yes, teacher," he agreed hoarsely. "I believe it's time for some private tutoring!"

A few moments later, heads turned along the highway as a bright pink car made its way swiftly down the road.

*   *   *   *   *

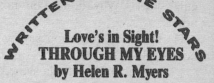

EVAN
Diana Palmer

Diana Palmer's bestselling LONG, TALL TEXANS series continues with EVAN....

Anna Cochran is nineteen, blond and beautiful—and she wants Evan Tremayne. Her avid pursuit of the stubborn, powerfully built rancher had been a source of amusement in Jacobsville, Texas, for years. But no more. Because Evan Tremayne is about to turn the tables...and pursue her!

Don't miss EVAN by Diana Palmer, the eighth book in her LONG, TALL TEXANS series. Coming in September...only from Silhouette Romance.

SRLTT

Take 4 bestselling love stories FREE

Plus get a FREE surprise gift!

Special Limited-time Offer

Mail to
Silhouette Reader Service™
3010 Walden Avenue
P.O. Box 1867
Buffalo, N.Y. 14269-1867

YES! Please send me 4 free Silhouette Romance™ novels and my free surprise gift. Then send me 6 brand-new novels every month, which I will receive months before they appear in bookstores. Bill me at the low price of $2.25 each—a savings of 25¢ apiece off cover prices. There are no shipping, handling or other hidden costs. I understand that accepting the books and gift places me under no obligation ever to buy any books. I can always return a shipment and cancel at any time. Even if I never buy another book from Silhouette, the 4 free books and the surprise gift are mine to keep forever.

215 BPA AC7N

Name	(PLEASE PRINT)
Address	Apt. No.
City	State	Zip

This offer is limited to one order per household and not valid to present Silhouette Romance™ subscribers. Terms and prices are subject to change. Sales tax applicable in N.Y.

SROM-BPA2DR

© 1990 Harlequin Enterprises Limited

Coming Soon

Fashion A Whole New You.
Win a sensual adventurous
trip for two to Hawaii via
American Airlines®, a
brand-new Ford Explorer
4 × 4 and a $2,000
Fashion Allowance.

Plus, special free gifts* are yours to
Fashion A Whole New You.

From September through November, you can take part in
this exciting opportunity from Silhouette.

Watch for details in September.

* with proofs-of-purchase, plus postage and handling